AUTUMN AT THE CORNISH GARDEN CAFÉ

Come to Cornwall and spend some time at the charming Cornish Garden Café. Surrounded by a beautiful, peaceful garden, the café is a haven at any time of the year. Breathe in the clean sea air, listen to the waves crashing against the shore and relax while you sip a refreshing drink and enjoy a tasty bite to eat...

Bookstore owner, Rosa Lake, is relieved that her divorce has been finalised. She hopes she'll be able to get on with her life now and to put the pain and uncertainty of the past decade behind her.

Primary school teacher, Henry Clay, has moved to the picturesque Cornish village to start his new job at the local school. After a change of career, he's excited to embrace this fresh start.

Henry is an avid reader and when he wanders into the bookstore one day, Rosa can't wait to serve him. Their mutual love of reading sparks something between them and soon they're aware that their friendship could turn into something more.

But Rosa and Henry have secrets in their pasts, and they struggle to share them. Will they find a way to overcome their differences, or will they agree to go their separate ways as the autumn leaves begin to fall?

1

ROSA LAKE

Taking a deep breath, Rosa Lake unlocked the door of The Book Nook and stood back. Her heart was racing, and her palms were clammy, but it was with excitement and not fear because the opening day of her bookshop in the Cornish village of Porthpenny had arrived. She had decided to open at 4 p.m. to allow people to browse around while enjoying some refreshments, asking any questions they may have and buying some books.

She turned towards the counter and leant against it, letting her gaze sweep over the space that had taken nearly three months of sweat and tears to transform. The shop hadn't been in terrible shape when she'd bought it, but had needed some updates — new shelving, a fresh coat of paint and new light fittings. Thankfully, the wiring was sound, and both the customer toilets and small staff kitchen were in good condition. The flat above the shop had only needed a touch of paint to brighten it up. Now filled with Rosa's things, it felt warm, lived-in — like home.

'Don't look so worried!' Vinnie Russo shook his dark head as he walked towards her. 'You're as pale as a ghost and that will scare the customers away.'

'I'm OK,' Rosa said.

'No, you're not! You need some bubbly inside you.' Vinnie reached for a bottle from the table near the door and popped the cork, shooting it up in the air. It dropped to the floor and bounced under a bookshelf. 'We'll find that one later.' He shrugged, then poured the bubbly into a flute. 'Here.'

He held the flute out, and Rosa eyed it warily.

'I don't know.' She nibbled at her bottom lip. 'I need to stay sober.'

'Darling Rosa, half a glass of bubbly won't hurt you. Besides'— he frowned at the bottle — 'It's Prosecco, not champagne, so you'll be fine.'

'There's no difference, really,' she said. 'The alcohol percentage is the same.'

Vinnie kept his hand holding the glass extended, so Rosa gave in and accepted it.

'There is a difference — according to my papa. But if he comes in here today, don't get him started on that topic. Like a bulldog with a bone, he is, when you get him going on one of his favourite rants.'

'Right. Thanks. I'll bear that in mind.' Rosa hadn't been formally introduced to Vinnie's papa but had heard some stories about him since she'd employed Vinnie. Mr Russo senior sounded intimidating, to say the least. He was a strong-minded patriarch who liked things done a certain way and that, apparently, was Enzo Russo's way.

'Get it down you.' Vinnie made a swigging motion with his free hand, then he picked up another flute and filled it before setting the bottle back in the container of ice. 'Mmmm. Not bad.' He nodded after taking a long drink. 'It'll do the job, anyway.'

While Vinnie sipped his drink, Rosa wandered around the shop, checking everything looked exactly how she'd imagined. Rosa had arranged the shelves by genre and then alphabetically by the authors' surnames. Tables showcased new releases and offers. A children's section boasted beanbags and a book vending machine. Finally, there was a vintage section, stocked with pre-loved books Rosa had sourced from antique shops, car boot sales, and house clearances. She hated to think of any books going to landfill and so if they could be saved, and given a new life and a new home, then she intended to rescue them and sell them in her shop. She had set up a website, and listed the books on there too, so buyers from all around the world could order anything that appealed to them. Rosa had also had a drinks machine installed, offering tea, coffee, and hot chocolate for customers to enjoy as they browsed or settled into one of the armchairs she'd placed throughout the shop. She had pictured a bookshop that would be well stocked, comfortable and welcoming, and wanted it to be a haven where villagers could go to find their next read or to track down a favourite book from their childhood. After working at a library and a bookshop in Bath before moving here, her dream of owning her own bookshop had come true, and The Book Nook was everything she'd wanted it to be and more.

Fairy lights twinkled around the glass of the windows and door, as well as around the shelves and counter. Posters of bookish quotes adorned any free wall space, and the scents of coffee and books permeated the air — a delightfully comforting and uplifting smell that Rosa had always adored.

Taking a sip of her drink, Rosa lowered her shoulders. Vinnie had been right, and the alcohol was helping her to relax as it took the edge off her tension.

'Look out!' Vinnie waved at the window and Rosa looked over to see a man gazing through the glass. 'Our first customer arrives!' Vinnie blew a pretend trumpet, then slipped behind the counter. He plastered on his signature grin, flashing the pearly white teeth he was proud of, and that Rosa knew were — unusually these days — all natural.

The man pushed open the door and stepped inside, and Rosa held her breath as he walked towards the counter.

'Hello,' he said, smiling.

Rosa opened her mouth, but nothing came out. She felt a prodding in her back, and then Vinnie whispered, 'Speak!'

'Oh … Hello!' She forced her lips into a smile. What was wrong with her? Surely being this nervous wasn't good for business. 'Sorry about that. I'm … so glad you joined us for our grand opening.' She gestured around the shop with both hands like a member of cabin crew showing him where the exits were, then realised what she was doing and dropped them to her sides.

Vinnie went to the table of refreshments, filled a flute, then brought it over to the man. 'Welcome to The Book Nook. I'm Vinnie and this nervous Nellie here is Rosa. She's the owner.'

'Hello Rosa and hello Vinnie.' The man accepted the flute of Prosecco. 'Thank you. I'm Henry Clay.'

'Hello Henry Clay.' Vinnie was staring hard at Rosa, but she couldn't take her eyes off Henry. She hadn't seen him around the village in the three months she'd been here, so perhaps he was a tourist or just passing through. He could be a holiday homeowner or here in the village on business. 'Rosa!' Vinnie dragged her attention back to the room.

'Henry. It's so good to meet you. And you are our first customer, which is very exciting. Feel free to browse around and let us know if you have any questions or if there's anything you'd like us to order in.' Rosa flashed another shaky smile, then walked around the counter and pretended to straighten some bookmarks.

'Enjoy the drink and help yourself to another when you're ready,' Vinnie said. 'Also, help yourself to the food.'

'Thank you. That's very kind,' Henry replied.

Vinnie came to Rosa's side and leant close. 'What is wrong with you?'

She glanced up at him, expecting to see annoyance, but he was frowning quizzically while a smile played on his lips.

'Nothing,' she squeaked. 'I just got stage fright.'

'Stage fright be damned!' Vinnie shook his head. 'If that's how you treat customers, we need to get you some customer service training, girl!'

'It's not that.' Rosa looked around for her glass, spotted it, and took a swig. 'I'm just jittery.'

Vinnie's frown faded, and then he cupped his chin with his right hand as his eyes widened. 'It's because he's hot, isn't it?'

'What?'

'You fancy Henry Clay.'

'I do not.'

'You so do.' He clapped his hands together and Rosa winced. 'But darling, I'm sorry to tell you this … that man is far too good-looking to be straight.'

'I don't care if he's straight or not because I don't fancy him!' Rosa realised she'd shouted the words and looked over at Henry to see him glance away from the counter. 'Vinnie, I am thirty-five and I recently moved to this gorgeous little village to escape all that nonsense. I just want to run my bookshop, read books, walk on the beach and catch up on all the sleep I missed over the past few years. I'm exhausted and just want some time to be me and to relax.'

'OK, honey, I get that.' Vinnie rubbed her arm. 'And you deserve to relax and read and enjoy your life again. I don't know all the details of what happened to you back in Bath, but you have told me you went through the mill. Please know that I'm here for you, whatever you need. And don't worry about Mr Clay because, as I said, he's more into men, I'm sure of it.'

'Good.' Rosa nodded. 'Now … It looks like we have more customers so I'm going to greet them while you check on Mr Clay.'

'It'll be my pleasure.' Vinnie patted his hair, then winked at Rosa before sashaying over to where Henry was browsing the biography section. Rosa watched as Vinnie charmed their first customer, then she turned her attention to the new arrivals.

The afternoon and evening flew past, and before Rosa knew it, the customers had eaten all the refreshments, and she'd made several pleasing sales. She'd recognised some customers as people from around the village, but while she knew some of them by name, others were familiar because she'd seen them in passing. Her friend Sita, who she'd known since her childhood holidays in the village, had come in with her family and that had been lovely. Since she'd bought the shop in Porthpenny, she'd worked hard to get it right before opening. She hadn't really integrated into the community yet — she'd been too busy and, she now realised, simply trying to find her feet. Moving from Bath to Cornwall had been a big step and a scary one, but she'd got to a point in her life where she'd felt that she had to change something. Moving was that change, along with another one that still made her heart ache at times, and at others made her hackles rise. That was the thing with being hurt by someone you loved. It took time to get past that and she was, she knew, grieving. Didn't they say that there were different stages of grief that a person had to work through? Rosa was certain that she was working through those stages even ten months on from deciding to move and start over.

'And that's a wrap!' Vinnie said as he locked the door and turned to face Rosa. 'Well done, darling.'

'Thank you.' Rosa walked over to him and peered out through the glass. The streetlights illuminated the scene, and the moon shone above the harbor, casting its silvery light across the water and the anchored boats. 'I couldn't have asked for a better view than this.'

'It's really something, right?'

'It really is.'

Vinnie wrapped an arm around her shoulders. 'You did brilliantly. The shop will be a roaring success and you'll have people visiting from far and wide to purchase your special editions or to sit and read for a while as they watch the world go by.'

'I hope so. I like your vision.' Rosa smiled up at him. 'Do you know what?'

'What?'

'I have a bottle of the good stuff upstairs in my fridge that I was keeping for today to celebrate. Do you fancy a glass?'

'I'm up for more Prosecco!' Vinnie grinned.

'Actually, it's champagne that I bought for us to share. I wanted to say thank you for all your hard work while we set the shop up. You've been awesome and I couldn't have done it without you.'

Vinnie pursed his lips. 'You probably could have, but it wouldn't have been as much fun.'

'Definitely not as much fun.'

She gave Vinnie a quick hug, then walked through the shop, *her* shop, and opened the door that led to the staffroom and another doorway that led to the flat upstairs. She loved Vinnie's prediction for the shop and hoped that, with him at her side, she could make it a roaring success. Her life to date hadn't been a roaring success but she was crossing everything that from this point on, things were about to change for the better.

Her aunt had always said *Home isn't a place. It's where you find the hearts that hold you when you fall.*

Rosa hoped with all her heart that she was finally home.

2

HENRY CLAY

*W*aking in a pool of sweat was not the way Henry had envisaged today starting, but the nightmare had been horrid, and he was glad to escape its clutches. Sometimes real life was horrifying enough to leave people scarred and there was no need for nightmares about zombies and other monsters. His nightmare had centred on the London boardroom where he'd spent so much time dealing with clients and businesses, sometimes feeling he'd have to sell his soul to reach a satisfactory solution. And then, of course, there had been other things that he'd felt trapped by, but those he'd prefer not to dwell on right now on the first day at his new job.

Stripping off his damp T-shirt and shorts, he changed into his running gear, grabbed his key, and let himself out of his cottage. He did a quick warmup, then set off towards the hill that led up to The Garden Café and the coastal path beyond.

He breathed deeply as he climbed the incline, his feet pounding the ground in their trainers, his body loosening as he let go of the nightmare and eased into movement. There was nothing like running for purging difficult emotions. It freed him to exist in the moment and allowed him to clear his mind, which was what he needed before his first day at the local primary school.

The sun rose over the sea, bathing the sky in lavender and peach hues. He passed the café gardens, then ran along the coastal path; the sea spread out to his right like a navy velvet blanket—cold, dark and deep beyond comprehension.

Checking his smart watch, he saw that he'd run over three kilometres and had just over an hour to get ready, so he turned and ran back the way he'd come. When he reached the village, the sky was lighter, and the air was fragrant with aromas of bread and pastries from the bakery and with a hint of wood smoke. It was very different from Reading, where he'd grown up and gone to university, and London, where he'd worked first in finance and then as a teacher, and it was a welcome change. Without this change, he'd worried he'd stay there all his life and never experience something different, like working in a village school. He was thirty-six, which was still young, but forty was looming and he didn't want to get to fifty and find that he hadn't done all the things he'd dreamt of doing. So here he was, taking a leap of faith and starting over in Cornwall.

He jogged towards the bookshop he'd visited yesterday as if drawn there by a mysterious force. Henry had always been an avid reader, and he loved browsing bookshops, so knowing there was one in the village excited him. He suspected Rosa and Vinnie would see a lot of him.

Slowing down, he paused in front of The Book Nook and peered through the window. The shelves and tables of books filled him with joy because within their pages, there were worlds he'd not yet discovered, and things to learn that would fill his mind and his days.

He looked down at his watch to check the time, and when he looked back up, he spotted Rosa smiling at him through the glass. His heart gave a little jump and reminded him of how he'd felt last night when he'd first seen her. With her white-blond hair with purple streaks that fell to her waist, her amber eyes, and pretty face, she'd been very pleasant to look at and he'd had to try not to stare. A pretty face did not easily sway Henry these days, but Rosa was a true beauty. Not in a conventional way, perhaps, but in a unique way, and he thought she was enchanting.

Rosa opened the door and came outside. 'Good morning.'

'Morning.'

'You've been running?' she asked, her eyes flicking over his attire.

'Yeah. It gets me started for the day and it helps me shake off bad dreams.'

'You too, huh?'

'Sorry?'

'You suffer from nightmares?' Her eyes held his, and he wondered how they were such an unusual colour. They were coppery yellow-brown with a warm, honey-like hue that made him think of warm summer days.

'I do. And you?'

'Unfortunately.' She shrugged. 'It makes getting out of bed in the mornings easier. I'm hoping that settling here will help with them, though.'

'Me too.'

They stood smiling at each other and then Rosa said, 'Would you like a coffee?'

'Oh, I … uh…' Henry looked down at his shorts and T-shirt. 'I'm a bit sweaty.'

'I can pour it into lidded mugs and we can take it down to the harbour and sit on a bench if you prefer. Only if you have time, though.'

Henry paused for a moment, then nodded. 'Coffee would be great.'

'Wonderful! I'll be back soon.'

Rosa went inside the bookshop and when she returned, she held out a reusable mug. 'I forgot to ask if you like sugar and milk.'

'Black is great.'

He accepted the mug, and Rosa locked the door then they strolled down to the harbour and sat on a bench. The landscape was a rich tapestry of late summer as it clung on and early autumn creeping in to cloak the village with her colourful changes.

'How long have you been in the village?' Rosa asked, turning on the bench so she was facing Henry.

'Only for a month. I bought a cottage but was waiting for the contracts to be finalised. There was a delay as the seller was in a chain and the house they were buying fell through, but then they found another one. Lucky for me.'

The gentle breeze caressed Rosa's long hair and the morning sunlight made it glow like spun silver. With the purple streaks that looked more lavender in this light, her hair made him think of sunrises he'd seen here in Cornwall and her amber eyes were as golden as the sunsets had been.

'That was lucky. Selling a property can be a trial in itself.'

'Did you sell one too in order to move here?' he asked.

'I did, but it wasn't mine. Well, legally it was, but it wasn't my home, it was my aunt's. I lived there growing up but… Well, it's a long story that I won't bore you with because I'm sure you're busy…' She sighed.

'I'd love to hear it but if it's a long one, I probably won't have time this morning as I start my new job.'

'You do?'

'I'm so nervous.' He let out a self-conscious laugh.

'What is it? Your new job?'

'I'm a teacher and I start at the village primary school today.'

'That's amazing.' Rosa smiled and his stomach flipped over. 'You must be very clever.'

'Ha! I'm not sure about that, but I do work hard. Most teachers do. Too hard sometimes, but it's the nature of the job. Although having said that, my quality of life is better now than it used to be when I worked in finance.'

'Was that in London?'

'It was. Not a lifestyle I miss or ever want to endure again.' He shuddered. 'I put in long hours as a teacher, but I also have a life. But when I worked in finance, that was my life. Most of it, anyway.' He sipped his coffee to prevent himself from saying more about what his life had involved back then. They were not details he'd care to share with Rosa in their first proper conversation. Just like her, he had things in his past that required time to explain, and first thing in the morning before work was not the right time.

He gazed at the boats bobbing in the harbour, their hulls weathered with salt and rust. The early rays of the sun turned the small ripples in the water into a glinting mosaic of gold and copper. Somewhere nearby, a dog barked, and another one answered while further away a cockerel crowed. The air smelled of dried seaweed and weathered rope, damp wood and engine oil, and the lingering earthy trace of mud exposed at low tide.

'I'm glad you got to do something else then,' Rosa said.

'What about you?' He drained his coffee mug and set it on the bench between them. 'How long have you lived here?'

'Three months. I sold my aunt's home and moved here to start over.' She lifted her chin and something flickered across her face like an aftershock. 'I mean … to open the bookshop and to have a fresh start.'

'Well, here's to fresh starts in Porthpenny!' Henry held up his empty mug and tapped it against hers. 'Let them be filled with adventures and many happy days.'

'To new adventures and happy days,' she said, holding his gaze.

Henry looked down at his watch. 'Oh man, I'd better get going if I'm going to shower and grab some breakfast before work. I'm so sorry.'

'Don't be. You don't want to be late for your first day.'

'I'm quite anxious now.'

'You'll be amazing. Don't doubt yourself.'

'Thank you. For the coffee and the kindness.'

'It's my pleasure. Have a wonderful day. I need to get back to the shop to prepare for my first full day, too.'

'Of course you do! Good luck with that.'

They both stood, and Henry held out the mug. 'Thanks again for that delicious coffee.'

'Anytime, Henry.'

'I'll see you soon.'

They stood gazing at each other for a few moments as the boats creaked and groaned as they shifted with the tide in the harbour and a gull circled above, its white wings catching the light. The briny tang of the sea seemed to envelop them, and Henry felt something washing over him. Something he hadn't experienced in years. He felt a strong sense of hope that living here and embracing this fresh start was going to be a positive thing for him and for Rosa.

'See you,' she said.

Henry turned and walked away, fighting the urge to turn back to catch one more glimpse of Rosa. Wondering if she really did remind him of a mermaid that had emerged from the sea to share the start of this new day with him.

3

ROSA

A week and a half had passed since Rosa had opened the bookshop and she was settling into the new routine of waking early, having breakfast, then heading downstairs to prepare the shop for the day ahead. Vinnie was a star of an employee, and she enjoyed his company and his ideas for displays and ways of increasing footfall.

Today he'd gone to his mum's for his lunch break, so Rosa was alone in the shop. She was browsing a catalogue from a publisher for upcoming titles when a shadow fell across the floor. Looking up, she saw an elderly man peering through the window, his face pressed close to the glass.

He raised a hand when he spotted her then came inside the shop.

'Good morning, young lady,' he said, removing his checked flat cap to reveal a shiny bald head.

'Good morning!' Rosa gave her customer a warm smile.

'I can't tell you how delighted I am that there is a bookshop in our village at last.' He folded his cap and tucked it into his blazer pocket. 'I've been wishing for one to open up here for years.'

'Well, I'm very happy to hear that.' Rosa came around the counter and held out her hand. 'I'm Rosa.'

'Hello Rosa.' He took her hand between both of his and she noticed how cold his hands were, how weathered by time and life the skin was. 'It's a pleasure to make your acquaintance. I'm Christopher Robin.'

She frowned uncertainly, not sure if he was teasing her.

'Yes, I know, but it's the name my parents gave me. It has raised some eyebrows and smiles over the years.' He gave a small laugh. 'There was no deliberate link to the famous books, though.'

'It's a wonderful name.'

'Thank you. I must say, this shop is delightful.' He let go of her hand and looked around. 'And it smells divine, a bit like a café.'

'That's the coffee machine.' Rosa gestured at the refreshments corner. 'Would you like a warm drink?'

'Oh!' He looked surprised. 'That would be very kind of you.'

'Come with me.' She led the way to the machine and showed him how it worked, then handed him a cup. 'Have whatever you like. And there are biscuits too.'

Christopher selected a coffee and a packet of shortbread biscuits, then Rosa told him to take a seat and relax for a bit. After feeling how cold his hands were, she wanted him to have the opportunity to warm up a bit.

While Christopher sat down, she returned to the counter and made some notes about books she'd like to order, then she checked the online orders on the computer behind the counter. When she looked over at Christopher, he was just finishing his drink.

'Would you like another?' She walked over to him.

'No, thank you, dear girl. That was perfect.'

'Were you looking for any books in particular?' she asked. 'Or just browsing.'

He stood up and shook his head. 'I'm actually here to find out if you would be interested in some books I have at home. Not to buy from me.' He held up a finger. 'To take off my hands. You see, my wife and I were always avid readers and we have a very well-stocked library at home. However, with her being gone and me getting older by the day, I'm trying to clear out a bit. I can't take it all with me now, can I?'

'You lost your wife?' Rosa asked.

'Two years ago. Nothing sinister, just old age. I always said to her I wanted to go first, but sadly she denied me that and went before me.' He held up his cup and the biscuit wrapper. 'What should I do with these?'

'There's a bin and recycling tub in the corner but I can sort them for you.' Rosa took the recycling from him, then came back to his side. 'I am so sorry for your loss.'

'Thank you but it's to be expected when one reaches their eighties or nineties. My dear Dolly was eighty-nine and I am now ninety-two.'

'That's amazing. I hope I look as good as you if I ever get to ninety-two.'

Christopher laughed. 'I'm sure you will look a million times better should you reach your nineties. It may sound like a great age to be, but I feel like I'm still twenty-one in my heart and mind. Other parts of me creak, groan and ache like I'm an old boat washed up after a storm though. The years fly past and I feel like my life has passed in the blink of an eye.'

A swell of emotion tightened Rosa's throat, and she coughed as she tried to dispel it.

As if emerging from a trance, Christopher shook his head and then placed a hand on her arm. 'Excuse me, dear. I don't mean to drift. I came here to speak to you about some books I have. Do you think you'd be interested?'

'I have a pre-loved and vintage books section here, so I'd certainly like to take a look if that's OK?'

'It is indeed.' Christopher nodded. 'When would you like to come and look? I'm pretty flexible these days. My social life is quite limited now.'

'I could come tomorrow. Would that work for you?'

'Absolutely.' He pulled a mobile phone from his pocket and said, 'Could you put your number in here and I'll text you? That way you can let me know when's a good time.'

Rosa did as he asked, then handed the phone back to him. 'Text me your address, too.'

'I'm not far away. Just along the road, past the school, then the row of cottages, and my home is the detached house on the left.'

'Thank you.'

'I shall see you tomorrow, then.' He tucked the phone in his trouser pocket, then got his cap out and put it on. 'And thank you again for the coffee and biscuits.'

'My pleasure, Christopher. See you soon.'

Rosa opened the door for him, then watched as he ambled away. For a man in his nineties, he was remarkable and so polite. She wondered if he managed all right living alone and if he had any relatives nearby to help him, should he require support. Life could be lonely at any age, especially if you'd lost your partner and had no friends around.

'I'm back!' Vinnie sang as he entered the shop carrying a paper bag. 'Oh, was that Christopher I saw leaving?'

'It was.'

'Bless his heart. Hasn't been the same since he lost his wife.'

'He seems lovely.'

'He is.' Vinnie placed the paper bag on the counter, then removed his jacket. 'But he keeps to himself. It's like he's afraid of being seen as a burden by anyone.'

'That's such a shame.' Rosa wrapped her arms around her waist. 'He's invited me to his house tomorrow to see if we want any of his books for the shop.'

'Get you! He must have taken a shine to you to invite you to the manor house.'

'Manor house?' Rosa frowned.

'That's what we call it round here. He lives in this big old house that he apparently built years ago. He's ... or he *was*... a talented carpenter. Such a shame though that they had that beautiful big house and couldn't have the children they wanted to fill it. I remember hearing my mama talking about it when I was younger. She said the Robins wanted children but couldn't have any and so they rattled around that house alone. Not that children are essential to happiness, of course, but if people want them, then it's sad if they can't have them.'

Rosa nodded. She understood that feeling all too well.

'From what I've heard, and I'm not one to gossip…' Vinnie put his jacket on the counter next to the bag, then placed his hands on his hips. 'There's a niece in Canada who'll inherit the estate after Christopher passes away.'

'I wonder if she'll come here to live.'

'I doubt it. But she'll be well off when that house sells for sure.' Vinnie raised his brows. 'Hopefully that's a long way off, as Christopher is the sprightliest ninety-something I've ever met. Not that I've met many people in their nineties, mind.'

'It's a great age.'

'It is.' Vinnie reached for the paper bag. 'Mama sent you some lunch.'

'Ooh! She didn't need to do that.'

'She said you're too skinny and you need some treats.'

'I love she thinks I'm skinny, even though she's mistaken about it.' Rosa laughed. 'What did she send me?'

'Sundried tomato brioche, pecorino cheese, Nocellara olives, and some pistachio cannoli.'

'Oh wow. She's so kind.'

Vinnie handed her the bag, then picked up his jacket again.

'I'll put this in the staffroom, then make us a coffee and you can tell me what we're ordering from that catalogue.'

'Great idea.'

Rosa opened the bag and gazed inside it, her mouth watering at the delicious treats it contained. Small acts of kindness could make such a difference to someone's day, and she was always grateful for them when they came her way.

The next day, Rosa, and Vinnie opened the shop and at ten o'clock, she set off for Christopher's home in her van. The white van bore the shop's name on the side, and Rosa felt a swell of pride every time she got behind the wheel. She had built this business alone and there was no one to thank for it but herself. Once upon a time, she'd been told — by a man — she was a dreamer who would never achieve her goals, but now she was living a life that resulted from her dreams and determination.

She drove through the village, past the school and the row of fishing cottages and then along a quiet country lane before pulling up outside the large, detached house that Christopher had told her about. She cut the engine and got out of the van, then walked to the front gate.

Surrounded by hedges, the four-storey grey stone house was double fronted with large bay windows, a wooden front door complete with a lion head brass knocker, and a spacious front garden. Pots lined the path from the gate to the front door, but they were empty or filled with weeds; one was smashed, and brown earth oozed from the hole like dried blood. Mole hills dotted the overgrown lawn, rising like dark acne on the green.

When she got close to the house, she could see that the paint was peeling around the windows and the glass was dirty. Christopher had been smartly dressed yesterday in his pressed trousers, shirt, cardigan and blazer, so she thought he must be a proud man. The state of his front garden suggested that he may be struggling to stay on top of everything, and her heart ached for him. In that moment, she knew she would do what she could to help him — as long as he was happy to have her assistance.

She raised the lion's head and knocked on the door then waited for Christopher to answer. Barking came from inside and then she heard footsteps and the door swung inwards.

'Ahhhh … morning, Rosa.' Christopher smiled at her and a small dog that she recognised as a Jack Russell ran past Christopher's legs and jumped up at her. 'Bobby! Get down now.'

Bobby stopped bouncing and ran back inside and Christopher apologised for his exuberance, then said that the dog was happy to have a visitor.

'He seems lovely,' Rosa said as Christopher invited her inside.

'Oh he's a friendly little chap, but he gets very excited.' Christopher closed the door and held a hand out. 'Come through to the kitchen and I'll make us a drink, then I'll take you to the library.'

'Sounds good to me.'

Rosa followed her host through the hallway, past a central staircase and into a large kitchen that wouldn't have seemed out of place in one of the historical dramas on TV. And while Christopher made tea, she made a fuss of Bobby, who brought her ball after ball, dropping them at her feet as if he was auditioning for a role courtside at Wimbledon.

4
HENRY

ithin a week, Henry felt he had settled in well at the village primary school. This school differed from his London school; it was smaller, and its pupils were village children, not city children. Of course, they were all children, but some of their life experiences to date had been different. The children in Porthpenny seemed more relaxed if anything and he wondered if that was because they lived near the sea in a small, friendly village. He felt more relaxed there, freer; he thought, and it was because he could head down to the beach and walk along the sand, gaze out at the seemingly endless horizon and breathe deeply of the salty air. London had sometimes overwhelmed him; here, he found a welcome tranquility.

He'd dismissed his class for break and was tidying his classroom before he had his planning and preparation time. Another teacher would take the pupils in his class for their PE session while he caught up with planning and marking. He also had a meeting scheduled with an external advisor about literacy, something he was passionate about. He felt happy — happy to be in Porthpenny, happy to be teaching at this lovely little school, and happy in general.

Of course, there were other things in London that had made him long to move away, to escape somewhere he could be anonymous and where no one knew about his past. Not that everyone in London had done, but there were people there who knew him and knew what had happened to him. People who knew *her*, and that had been tough. A shiver ran down his spine and he wriggled his shoulders, then rubbed at the back of his neck. He didn't want to bring those memories here to this fresh start. Instead, he gazed out of the window at the playground, where the leaves on the trees were turning shades of orange, red and brown. Those that had already fallen skittered across the grass, lifted and teased by a gentle autumn breeze. Autumn was a season of change, of quiet transformation — and Henry believed it could bring change for him too, here in this village, in this school. Now, he could be the person he aspired to be, free from the future his father had once envisioned for him — and from the one *she'd* wanted for him. Trying to live up to people's expectations never went well and often led to their disappointment and sometimes a sense of failing people that left a sour taste on his tongue.

'Knock! Knock!'

Henry turned to see Pete Malik standing in the open doorway holding two mugs.

'Morning,' he said. 'Come on in.'

Pete was the Year 4 teacher, and he'd been very kind to Henry since he started at the school, telling him he was there to answer any questions he had or to provide any support he may need.

'Got you a coffee.' Pete held out one of the mugs.

'Thanks. That's very kind of you.'

'Pleasure.' Pete smiled. 'How are things?'

'Great.' Henry nodded. 'I have PPA after break and a meeting with the literacy advisor. So lots to do, but it's all good.'

'There's always lots to do in this job.' Pete laughed. 'You should hear Naveen in the evenings. He's all like, "Pete, do you really have to do all that marking tonight? Can't we go out for food or to see a movie?" It's different for a mechanic though because he doesn't have to bring his work home with him.'

'Tell me about it.' Henry shook his head. He loved being a teacher but the workload could be overwhelming if it wasn't managed well. 'I try to draw a line and keep some time aside for actually living. But I'm single and I imagine it's harder if you have a partner and a family.'

'Naveen and I don't have children because he's enough work for me.' Pete winked. 'And yes, I try to make sure he gets enough of my time. Quality time, that is. Got to keep the husband happy, right?'

'I'm sure you do.' Henry laughed.

'Plus, I love teaching and shaping young minds so I wouldn't want to do anything else. Naveen is pretty good really, it's just now and then he'd like me to have less work to do outside of the school day. Anyway...' Pete pushed a hand through his light brown mullet. 'Do you need any help with anything?'

'I don't think so. I'm on top of things at the moment and hope to stay that way. September is always a nice term because everything's so fresh. The exercise books are clean and ready to be filled, the children's minds are clear from the summer holidays and they're ready to learn, and the weather is cooler, so my mind is too.'

Pete grinned. 'I feel like that about September term, too. After the summer, I'm ready to start again. Summer at the coast is special.'

'Too true.' Henry liked the thought of future summers in the village and how much he would enjoy going for an early morning swim and a run along the coastal path. Everything was here at his disposal and he intended to make the most of it all. 'I was thinking that perhaps we could arrange some outings to the bookshop for the children this term.'

'That would be a good idea.' Pete took a sip of coffee. 'Perhaps we can get some local businesses involved to donate book vouchers so they can all get something while they're there.'

'That would be brilliant. It could be a termly outing to encourage reading and develop literacy skills.' He had tried to suggest a similar scheme at his last school, but it had been shot down because of funding issues. This had made him sad, so he'd sent out emails to companies asking them to support the scheme. He'd raised some money, but with so many pupils, it wouldn't have gone far. Instead, he'd used the money to pay for transport to the closest library and the pupils had learnt about how they could join the library and take out books to read. Some of them had got really excited about visiting the library, which had warmed his heart. He'd been able to extend the scheme so it would continue after he left and he hoped they'd keep it going for the pupils because the school library hadn't been fit for purpose.

'Well, let's see what we can do then.' Pete raised his mug, and Henry tapped his gently against it.

'I'll speak to Rosa about it too,' Henry said thoughtfully.

'Rosa?' Pete asked.

'The owner of The Book Nook. She's very nice and—'

'Is that a blush I see in your cheeks?' Pete waggled his eyebrows.

'A blush?' Henry raised a hand and touched his cheeks and realised they were warm. 'I don't think so. Why would I be blushing?' Just trying to deny it made his cheeks grow hot, and a nervous chuckle slipped out.

'Is this bookshop owner attractive, then?' Pete tilted his head.

'Rosa's very nice. She's welcoming and book mad and … and … I guess she's attractive. But I wouldn't know much about that, really.'

'Why not?' Pete's brows met above his nose. 'Oooh … Are you into men? If you are, I know some great single men. I could set you up on a date with any of them and—'

'No! Thanks. I'm not … I like women. But I'm not in the right place to date anyone. I'm … taking some time ….'

'No problem. Sometimes we all need a break from romance. But just so you know, if you do fancy dating again, I have friends who're single and ready to mingle. Male and female.' He winked.

'Thanks.' Henry took a sip of coffee and willed the blush to fade from his cheeks. What was he, thirteen? 'I'll bear that in mind.'

'Excellent!' Pete headed for the door. 'Well, break will be over soon, and I have a class to teach. Enjoy your PPA time and your meeting.'

'Cheers.'

After Pete had gone, Henry turned back to the window and gazed out at the landscape. After the past few years, he really wasn't in the right place to date again but he couldn't deny that he found Rosa intriguing. She was beautiful and sweet, and she loved books. What was there about her that was unlikeable? But then he'd been burnt before and found that how someone initially seemed could soon change once they felt comfortable with you. And he didn't want to end up in that type of situation ever again.

Staying single was for the best. Wasn't it?

5

ROSA

*C*hristopher's kitchen was enormous and could have fitted Rosa's whole flat inside it, but it was also homely. She sat at the large oak table while he made tea. He served the tea in bone china mugs and placed a plate of digestive biscuits on the table, then sat opposite her. Bobby climbed into a basket next to the Aga and curled up, his small head buried underneath his tail. He dropped off to sleep quickly while Rosa wrapped her hands around her mug and savoured the warmth of the tea and the kitchen. She felt relaxed and comfortable in Christopher's home, savoured the September morning sunshine coming through the large window.

'So what brought you to Porthpenny?' he asked as he stirred sugar into his tea.

'I was at a crossroads, and I needed to make some big decisions.'

'Oh, the old crossroads in life, eh?' He winked at her. 'I've been at a few of those myself over the years. Difficult at times, aren't they?'

Rosa nodded. 'I was … coming out of a difficult relationship and I needed to decide what came next. My aunt passed away and left me her house. Having grown up there, I didn't want to live there now … it was far too big for one person… so I sold it and looked for somewhere to live. I always dreamt of opening my own bookshop. A childhood friend of mine who lives in Porthpenny told me there was a shop for sale here with a flat above it, and I knew I had to see it.' She gave a small shrug. 'As soon as I did, I fell in love with it and that was that. Here I am.'

'There are worse places to live.' Christoper smiled. 'I've had a very happy life here, in all honesty. It's not the same without my wife, but I doubt I'll be hanging around long and so I try to make the most of my days. I'm trying to sort everything out now because I don't want to leave a mess for someone else to deal with.'

'You don't have any family around then?' she asked, aware of what Vinnie had told her, but not wanting to seem like she was assuming anything. There could be someone else around, surely? But then she thought of herself and how she had no one other than Sita. There was her father, but he was virtually a stranger so she couldn't exactly reach out to him for support. She'd considered it when things had got really bad but then she'd realised that it would seem odd to say, 'Hey, Dad, I know I haven't seen you in years because you emigrated to Australia with your second wife, but I'm really low at the moment and could do with your love and support. How does that sound?' He hadn't cared when she was a child and he wouldn't care now she was an adult, so it was better for her to manage alone and not to have any expectations of others. That way she wouldn't feel let down or hurt because feeling hurt was the worst, especially when the person who should have had your back above all others decided to lie to you in the very worst of ways.

'I don't, no,' Christopher shook his head. 'My wife and I couldn't have children. When we were trying, it was a long time ago and medicine wasn't as advanced as it is now. We didn't want to go through tests and possibly intrusive exam-inations and so we left it to fate. We had each other, and we felt lucky for that and so we spent our days loving each other and waiting to see what each month would bring. It never brought a child, sadly, as I know that for Dolly it would have meant the world. Not that I didn't want to be a father because I did, but Dolly wanted it with every fibre of her being. To feel a baby grow in her womb and then to hold that child in her arms was a dream she had from the moment we met.' He paused and took a sip of tea, his eyes watery when they met Rosa's again. 'It wasn't to be, though. With the passing of time, we gradually accepted it and tried to enjoy other things. There was Dolly's niece, of course, her sister's girl, but then her sister and brother-in-law emigrated to Canada and so we never saw the girl again. We could have travelled out there, but Dolly was afraid of flying and they never came back to the UK. And as much as Dolly loved her niece, she was someone else's daughter. In contrast to your situation because your aunt raised you, correct?'

'She did. She was my mother's sister. I lost my mother when I was six and my father had already gone to Australia by that point, so I had no one else.'

'I'm sure it was a pleasure for her to raise you.'

'You're very kind, Christopher, thank you. I don't know that my aunt felt she had a choice. She was a good woman though, and I had a happy childhood.'

'Did you feel you missed out at all? On having a father figure around?' he asked gently.

Rosa thought about the question. She'd considered it herself over the years, of course she had. 'Sometimes I wished he would turn up on the doorstep and tell me he loved me and was coming home to take care of me. But then I'd think about the reality of who he was and how he wasn't there for me over the years, and it hit me every time that my aunt was the person who loved me. She showed me how much she cared through what she sacrificed for me and I loved her for it.' Rosa's heart ached as she thought of how much she missed her aunt and how much she'd love to see her again. 'I lost her eighteen months ago and I miss her so much.'

'Grief is the price we pay for love.' Christopher shook his head and stared at his mug. 'But how dull life would be if we didn't love others. Love is a beautiful gift and finding love in another human being, whether romantic love or another form, is a wondrous thing indeed. I would suffer this pain of grief a million times over just to have my time with my wife again.'

Rosa swallowed hard. She understood this type of pain and grief. The pain of loving someone and losing them, even when her loss had been a different kind. At least for Christopher, losing his wife had been because of age and not because she had chosen to leave him. Rosa was coping with the pain of loss and the sting of rejection and betrayal. The end of her relationship had called into question everything she'd spent years trying to believe in, and it was hard to get past that. How did you trust even yourself when the person you'd put your faith in wasn't the person you'd believed them to be at all?

After they'd drunk their tea, he led her through the hallway. Pushing open a door, he revealed his library and Rosa was breathless at the beauty of it. French doors revealed a beautiful side garden where trees showed their autumn shades of gold, red, and brown. Floor to ceiling bookshelves showcased books, books, and more books. There was a desk against the inner wall and a chaise longue near the window with a small side table.

'Some books in here are recent releases but there are many older volumes that may be of interest to you.' Christopher pointed at some shelves where hardback books were lined up in size order with covers ranging from dark red to varying shades of brown and blue. 'Please feel free to have a good look.'

Rosa walked to the bookshelves and touched a hand reverently to the spines. She could see a complete set of novels by Charles Dickens and a set by Jane Austen. Choosing a novel, she took it from the shelf, admiring its pristine cover before carefully opening it. She raised it to her face and inhaled the beautiful old book smell. Placing it back on the shelf, she browsed more of the shelves and her heart rate increased as it always did when she was surrounded by books. She could comfortably while away days, weeks, and months reading in this room.

'I have a few things to do, so I'll leave you to see if there's anything you want here. I'll be in the kitchen if you need me.' Christopher went to the door.

'Wait!' Rosa turned to him. 'Are you sure about this? I mean … Are you sure you want to divide up this incredible library?

It seems such a shame. There's a lifetime of reading here, books you've collected and cared for like—' She pressed her lips together, aware of what she was about to say.

'Like children?' he asked, voicing her words. 'For Dolly, they were her children. Collecting books became her obsession. She suffered somewhat from anxiety and depression, but reading was her escape. If we'd had children, then she might have been different, I think. Instead, she found solace in reading and collecting books. I'd often return from work to find her curled up on the chaise near the window, the lamp on while the garden beyond lay in darkness. Over the years, we had cats and dogs and they'd keep her company and snuggle up with her.' His eyes glassed over as he remembered and Rosa listened, entranced by the image of the woman who'd once lived here and spent her days in this library. How sad that she hadn't been the mother she'd longed to be, but how wonderful that reading had provided her with comfort. 'We rarely watched TV and instead, we'd eat dinner, then I'd join her in here and sit at the desk reading or sorting through bills and business documents, while she'd read. Afterwards, before bed, we'd talk about what she'd read that day and she'd make me laugh with funny stories and make me cry with the sad ones. We marked every birthday and Christmas with more book purchases. If she was here still, she'd be in your shop daily and probably spend all our money there.'

'I wish she could visit the shop,' Rosa said. 'I would have loved to meet her.' And she would because Dolly sounded like someone she'd have got on with.

'She would have been the perfect employee for you when she was younger,' he said wistfully. 'She could have advised anyone on whatever reading material they were looking for.

Ah, my sweet girl.' He sighed. Rubbed at his eyes. 'Anyway, please take your time. I'll make more tea when you're done if you'd like?'

The hope in his voice made Rosa's heart squeeze. It was clear that Christopher would like her company for longer. 'That would be perfect, thank you.'

After he'd gone, she sent a quick text to Vinnie to let him know she'd be back later than anticipated, then she returned her attention to the shelves. There were many titles she knew would sell well and some that her online customers had already asked her to source, so she made notes about them on her phone. She could stock the books for Christopher, then sell them and pay him when each book sold. She couldn't afford to pay him outright for the titles, but she could facilitate their sale. Usually, this would be done for a small commission, but in this case, she simply wanted to help this lovely man sort out his affairs because he clearly needed assistance. Rosa would be that person and it would be her first good deed in this lovely Cornish village. People needed to help people more, she often thought, and she would be happy to help Christopher, especially if he shared more stories about the fascinating Dolly. The way his face lit up when he talked about his wife made it a pleasure to listen to him and Rosa knew that speaking about his wife was helpful for him because without sharing memories of our loved ones, how could we keep them with us?

6

ROSA

*J*ust over a week later, Rosa walked up to The Garden Café. Three weeks in, September was glorious in Cornwall. The trees around the village and in the surrounding fields blazed with tones of red, orange, and yellow. Summer was fading while autumn crept in with cool, crisp evenings and the rustle of leaves underfoot. The days still clung on to the last lingering warmth of summer, but the change in the air was unmistakable.

When she reached the gardens surrounding the café, she let herself in through the wooden gate and wandered around, admiring the apple and pear trees heavy with fruit and the blackberries, ripe and shiny, that grew in abundance on the bushes. Beneath the fruit trees, the grass was abundant with windfallen fruit the breeze had shaken from the branches or that had dropped under its own ripened weight. Some of the apples and pears had split, attracting insects to feast on their sweet fruit while others lay bruised but intact.

The flower beds were fading, but there were patches of colour where dahlias and chrysanthemums still bloomed. In the raised garden beds, pumpkins ripened — orange, pear-shaped, and yellow—while local farm pumpkins and squashes filled crates outside the café. Locally grown organic potatoes, carrots, parsnips, and onions were also for sale. Rosa noticed the small cardboard containers on a table ready for customers to fill with blackberries, apples, pears, and plums so they could take them home to enjoy the season's harvest.

When she went inside the café, the delicious aromas of coffee and pumpkin spice, of pastry and melted cheese struck her. Her stomach grumbled, and she knew she'd be taking something back to the shop for lunch for herself and Vinnie.

Small gold vases filled with corn stalks, dried lavender, and autumn leaves decorated the tables, and candles and pinecones adorned the windowsills. Behind the counter, the specials menu boasted a range of autumnal treats, including spiced butternut squash soup, cheesy leek and potato pie, apple and Cornish cheddar pasties and honey roasted root vegetable salad with a wild garlic pesto. Her mouth watered, and she wished she could sample everything on the menu. Alongside the main dishes was the dessert menu, and while she waited to be served, she browsed it, her appetite growing. Should she order apple and rhubarb crumble with custard, pecan pie with rich, golden crusted clotted cream, or spicy gingerbread with thick cream cheese frosting?

'Hello there.' Pearl Draper smiled at her from behind the counter, her short hair held back from her forehead with a gold scarf decorated with hedgehogs, her dark red crocheted jumper over a damask vest top. Her hazel eyes twinkled, and Rosa thought not for the first time that Pearl looked decades younger than her seventy-odd years. 'What do you fancy today, Rosa?'

'I'm not sure. It all looks so good.'

'An autumnal feast, right?' Pearl gestured at the kitchen. 'Ellie has created some crackers this month.'

'She definitely has.' Rosa nodded. 'I think I'll have to try the cheesy leek and potato pie.'

'Would you like that with salad or beans?'

'Baked beans?'

'Yes. They're organic and we make them here.'

'Oh go on then. That's the ultimate comfort food.'

'It is indeed. And how about to drink?'

'What would you recommend?'

Pearl frowned. 'To go with your lunch, I'd suggest the ginger tea. Will you want a dessert?'

Rosa laughed. 'I'm tempted but I feel like I'm being greedy. Perhaps I'll have my lunch then take dessert to go because I want to take something back for Vinnie too.'

'Sounds like an excellent plan to me.' Pearl nodded.

Rosa paid and located a vacant window table. She pulled out the chair and hung her jacket over the back, then sat down and got out her phone. She habitually scrolled through it, then flipped it over on the table and gazed out the window.

The colours of the garden were enchanting, and she watched as a squirrel hopped across the grass, picked up something, then turned it over in its small paws. Liking its find, it tucked it inside its mouth and jumped to the nearest tree, then darted up into the branches. Birds fluttered around, settling on the bird tables and feeders, tucking into the seeds and nuts that Pearl had put out for them. Fallen leaves carpeted the grass, and someone had swept piles against the hedges for recycling as garden waste.

'Here you go.' Pearl appeared with her drink, then returned with her food.

'Oh my goodness, that looks amazing!' Rosa licked her lips.

'Enjoy!'

Pearl walked away, and Rosa gazed at the plate of steaming food. The beans, mixed in size, were coated in a rich home-made tomato sauce, and a golden cheese topping covered the leeks and potatoes. She was going to want a nap after she'd eaten it all.

Half an hour later, her belly full, she went to the counter and ordered a few things to take away, then she put her jacket back on and left the café. The air seemed cooler than earlier, but she knew it was probably because she'd been inside the café's cosy interior. She'd paid for a box of blackberries, so she filled one up and tucked it into the paper bag of goodies she'd bought, then strolled along the path and out of the garden gate.

On her walk down to the village, she stopped and gazed out at the sea, shimmering gold in the afternoon light. She could hear a wood pigeon calling and somewhere out at sea an engine hummed. Being here in this perfect location was creating a sense of peace in her soul that she couldn't recall ever feeling before. She suspected people often talked about peace but seldom felt it, and she wanted to hold onto it while she could. She breathed in the briny air and held it in her lungs, then slowly released it, thanking the universe for bringing her to Cornwall, even if the route had been painful. At this point in time, she was where she belonged, and this brought her comfort. Yes, she had been through pain, but she was here now and the way ahead would hopefully be better than the way here had been.

She started walking again, her thoughts straying to her aunt who would have loved to come back to Porthpenny. They'd enjoyed holidays here when Rosa was younger and her aunt had loved the village and the surrounding countryside. They'd stayed at a local caravan park and at a rental cottage, and each holiday had been magical in the way that childhood holidays often are. She had memories of the sun on her skin, sand between her toes and the taste of salt on her lips. Of pony trekking and swimming, of clotted cream teas and lazy hazy days that made her heart ache for times gone by. They were times she would never possess again, but that would always remain in her heart, just like her aunt would.

Thoughts of her aunt, who had remained single for most of Rosa's life, made her think of Christopher and she found herself walking towards his home. The thought that he spent a lot of time alone had been on her mind, and she couldn't bear to think that he was lonely. He hadn't said as much, but he had lost his wife, his best friend and partner, and he must feel lonely sometimes. She would go to see if she could do anything for him and update him on the books of his she'd sold so far. She had the information in a folder she could access from her phone and she hoped Christopher would be pleased with the amount of money he'd made.

Outside his house, she sent Vinnie a message to say she wouldn't be long, then she knocked on Christopher's front door. The confusion when he opened the door that was supplanted by a wide smile made her chest ache and she was instantly glad she'd come.

'Hello, Rosa. To what do I owe the pleasure?' he asked as Bobby rushed out and circled her legs.

'I've been to the café for lunch and I thought I'd stop by on my way back to the shop.'

'How nice!' He smiled.

'Oh … Also, I brought you a few things. They sounded too good not to try.'

His eyes went to the paper bag, and his smile widened. 'Well, in that case, I'd better get the kettle on.'

As Rosa followed him through to the kitchen, she sent out a silent apology to Vinnie. She knew he had a lasagne in the fridge for lunch that his mother had made for him, so he wouldn't starve, and she'd go back and get him some more café goodies later on. For now, though, Christopher needed them more than Vinnie.

In the kitchen, she sat down and got the goodies out of the bag, then she made a fuss of Bobby. He rolled onto his back for her to tickle his belly, then he pawed at her legs so she lifted him onto her lap where he curled up and dropped off to sleep.

'He likes you,' Christopher said as he set two mugs of tea on the table. 'He doesn't do that with many people, so he must trust you. That's good.' He nodded as if something had been on his mind, but he turned and went to a cupboard, got out two plates and brought them to the table along with paper napkins.

'He's lovely.' Rosa stroked Bobby's soft fur and his small silky ears and he grunted in his sleep.

'He's a loyal little companion. I um … The thing about being left alone now is that I worry what will happen to him when I'm gone.'

'Don't say that! I'm sure you have years ahead of you yet.'

Christopher cleared his throat. 'Maybe. But I want to sort everything out so I can relax, you know? Clearing the house as much as possible and putting plans in place just in case … for when I …' He let the words hang in the air and Rosa sucked in a shaky breath. Yes, she knew, her aunt had been the same. Some people took out life insurance and funeral plans in their thirties and forties, but some people couldn't bear to think about a time when they wouldn't exist in the world. Some people found peace knowing their relatives wouldn't have to worry about funeral plans and costs; others preferred to believe they would eventually write a will, and often never did. It was difficult, but Rosa knew that for her aunt, with it being just the two of them, it had been important for her to know that Rosa would have a simple time of it after she'd gone. She'd been a stickler for organisation and so when she had passed, Rosa had known what she'd wanted and everything she'd had was left to Rosa in a very clear and concise will.

'I understand,' she said softly. 'My aunt was the same. She worried about leaving a mess for me and so she had everything spelt out in her will and after she passed, while sad, it was straightforward.'

'My niece deserves the same,' he said as he sat down opposite her. 'And so I shall sort it all out. However, as far as Bobby is concerned, I do worry. I'll ensure funds are available for him, so whoever adopts him after my death won't have to worry about veterinary bills or similar costs. Isn't that right, Bobby?' He gazed at the dog, his eyes filled with love.

Rosa's throat was aching now, and she opened her mouth to speak, but her vision blurred.

'I apologise.' Christopher shook his head. 'You came to visit with delicious baked goods and here I am upsetting you. I am so sorry for the loss of your aunt and for bringing back sad memories.'

'No … It's not… that.' Rosa coughed. 'It's seeing how much you love Bobby and thinking of him having to manage without you.'

'He will find another mum or dad to love him.'

'But he … he loves you.' Rosa said the words and realised she sounded like an innocent child with no idea of the harsh realities of the world. She had never been that child; her father had abandoned her and then she'd lost her mum so young. 'I mean … I can't bear the thought of him not having you.'

'Rosa … It's a big ask, but do you think you would…' He shook his head. 'No. It's too much to ask.'

'If you want to ask if I would take care of him should anything happen to you, then yes I would. In fact, I would be honoured to care for him. Of course I would. But nothing is going to happen to you for a long time and so we don't need to worry about that.'

'Of course not.' Christopher smiled, but there was something in his eyes that suggested he thought otherwise. 'Now shall we eat this feast because it looks incredible?'

'It's all for you,' she said. 'I had lunch already.'

'I couldn't possibly eat all this. Please have some of the desserts, at least?'

'OK then.' Rosa shrugged and giggled. She hadn't eaten dessert at the café, planning on trying some of the ginger cake when she got back to the shop, so now she helped herself to a slice while Christopher nibbled on a cheese and apple pasty then ate the crumble and clotted cream from the recyclable pot Pearl had packed them in.

They washed the food down with more tea and Christopher chatted about his niece in Canada and what he knew of her life there and Rosa listened, aware that having someone listen was probably nice for him. Plus, she found him fascinating, his deep voice and genteel tone, the way his eyes glossed over when he recalled a detail and how dimples appeared in his cheeks when he smiled. He must have been a handsome man when he was younger and she wondered what he had looked like and what his wife had been like too. Had they fallen in love, had eyes for no one else? Had theirs been a devoted marriage with no cruelty or heartbreak, the kind that only lucky people found?

'Ah, look at me, wittering on,' he said, shaking his head. 'I apologise yet again, Rosa. You have been very kind allowing me to take up so much of your time.'

'I'm enjoying myself,' she said.

'But you have a shop to run and I'm an old man taking up your afternoon. Please don't lose sales because of me.'

Rosa glanced at the clock and realised she'd been there for over an hour. She would need to get back to the shop, but she could spare ten more minutes. 'I will have to get back so

Vinnie can take his lunch break but first let me tell you about the books of yours I've already sold.' She got out her phone and opened the folder, then talked him through the numbers and was pleased to see his brows rise and a smile play on his lips.

'That's an excellent start,' he said.

'Would you like me to transfer the money to a bank account or to send it another way?' she asked.

'Oh no, I don't want the money,' he said.

'But it's yours. Of course you need the money.'

'I thought that I'd like to donate it to the local animal rescue sanctuary and, perhaps, if there's enough, to the village school literacy fund. I know they're always trying to raise money for the children, so how about you split it between the two?'

'That would be very generous of you, Christopher,' she said. 'Are you sure?'

'I'm sure.' He smiled. 'Now you should head back to work. But thank you so much for visiting. I can't tell you how much it means to me and to Bobby.'

As he pushed back his chair and stood, she noticed him grab the edge of the table and grip it, a whisper of pain crossing his features. His body seemed to hesitate, as if every movement cost him more than he would ever let on.

'Are you all right?' She set Bobby down gently in his basket, then went to Christopher's side, but he nodded and held up a hand.

'Absolutely fine, dear. Just a twinge of arthritis. All to be expected when you reach your nineties.'

Rosa paused for a moment, yearning to ask if he'd seen the doctor but not wanting to pry. She touched his arm. 'If you need anything, you have my number. Please call, anytime.'

'You are very kind, Rosa. Thank you again,' he said with a smile. 'And Bobby says thank you for the cuddle.'

Outside the front door, Rosa turned and looked at Christopher. The urge to hug him was strong, but she didn't know how he'd take it, so she gave a small wave instead and he waved back. As she walked along the path and out onto the pavement, her throat was tight and her eyes stung with tears. She had a feeling that Christopher wasn't telling her everything and despite knowing him for just a short time, she was already very fond of him. People could be lonely whatever age they were. She'd been there, but to be elderly and lonely was deeply sad. She would befriend Christopher and help him with whatever he needed. Her aunt had always taught her to reach out if people seemed in need of support and it was something Rosa had always done, even when her own heart had been broken into a thousand tiny pieces.

And as for little Bobby, the tiny dog had already won her over, so she would be there for him too. Come what may...

7

HENRY

*S*eptember had flown past and Henry was settled in his new routine. He'd decided that Saturday mornings were the perfect time to head to The Garden Café for breakfast to enjoy a treat or two.

It was cold out this morning, a proper autumnal day, with a brisk wind blowing in off the sea. The air was laced with salt and the earthy tones of fallen leaves along with the sweetness of wind-fallen fruit. Pale sunlight filtered through scattered clouds, its rays gently caressing the frothy waves. Gulls glided above, their calls carried on the wind like they were welcoming the autumn in and preparing for the winter ahead.

Henry had put on a warm jacket and a hat for his walk to the café and enjoyed the sensation of the cool air enveloping him while he walked. He loved being outdoors and found it a great way to blow off the cobwebs and to clear his mind. He had some schoolwork to do over the weekend, but he'd fit it in around doing some things he enjoyed. Early in his teaching career, he's learnt the importance of balance to prevent burnout and maintain his effectiveness as a teacher.

When he reached the café, he ordered at the counter, then took a seat at a table near the window. Pearl's granddaughter, Ellie Cordwell, brought his breakfast over and they chatted for a bit. Ellie was in a relationship with a local man called Jasper Holmes, who had two young children at the primary school — Mabel and Alfie. Henry had seen them at the school and around the village and they seemed very happy together. Whenever he saw a loving couple, it gave him hope it was possible to be happy with someone and that relationships didn't have to be toxic.

He picked up the crusty roll and took a bite, then closed his eyes for a moment. The bacon was salty and crispy, the brie creamy and the cranberry sauce added the perfect tart yet sweet contrast. Henry rarely ate bacon because he knew it wasn't good for him, but this was a treat so he'd enjoy it.

'That good, eh?'

He opened his eyes to find Rosa smiling at him.

'Sooo good. I recommend this one if you're here for breakfast.'

'I am. I'm meeting my friend, so I'll consider ordering that…' She peered at the roll.

'It's bacon, brie, and cranberry.'

'It sounds delicious. Perhaps I'll take one to the shop for Vinnie too.' She glanced around and spotted a woman waving from the green leather sofa by the bookshelves. 'Ah, there's Sita.'

Henry smiled over at Rosa's friend, then took a sip of his caramel latte. Sita Vandermeer and her husband Niels also had children at the school, so he was getting to know quite a few of the villagers via their children. Wherever he went in the village, he was going to bump into parents or pupils, but he didn't mind because it was what he'd expect from a small community.

'Are you here alone?' Rosa asked.

'I am.'

'You could join us if you like?'

'I wouldn't want to intrude.' He smiled and shook his head. 'I've got a podcast to listen to and then I've got chores to do and errands to run. Thank you though. It's very kind of you to offer.'

'No problem.' She smiled again, and he felt bad, like he might have offended her by declining.

'Another time, perhaps? If you'd like to, that is.'

'Another time.' She nodded. 'Enjoy your breakfast and I'll see you soon.'

Before she could leave, his phone rang; he answered automatically then realised — too late — that it was his mother on FaceTime.

'Henry!' She waved out of the screen at him. 'Hello, darling. How are you?' Her eyes slid to Rosa, and she waved. 'Hello there! Oh … Sorry, darling, do you have company? Shall I call back later?'

'No, it's fine, Mum.' Henry turned to Rosa. 'Apologies.'

'No problem,' Rosa said. 'And hello, Henry's mum. Right, I'm going to order my food and leave you in peace.'

Rosa walked away, and Henry looked back at the screen. 'I'm actually in the café at the moment having breakfast and I don't want to be *that person* who takes a call while others are eating their breakfast, so shall I call you back?'

'All right, darling. But don't take long because I'm off to the WI cake sale at noon.'

'I'll be ten minutes.' Henry ended the call and stared down at his crusty roll. Sighing, he picked it up and ate quickly. His mum would want to know more about the mysterious woman she'd seen him with, and he knew she'd be pinning her hopes on Rosa being a *person of interest*. She was desperate to see him settled, as she always put it, and telling her he wasn't interested never seemed to convince her.

After he'd finished his breakfast, he took the plate and mug to the counter and thanked Ellie again. Then he left the café and walked through the gardens and up the slight incline to the bench that had an amazing view of the sea. There was a large oak tree behind the bench and autumn had painted the leaves in tawny gold and russet hues. Some lay on the ground around the bench like autumn confetti, while others hung on, rustling like crumpled paper in the sea breeze.

Henry got his phone from his pocket and scrolled to the last caller, then swiped to call his mum. The phone rang twice, then her face appeared on the screen, familiar and comforting as always with her grey bobbed hair with a blunt fringe, bright blue eyes behind red framed glasses and pearly pink lipstick. He knew she would smell like white musk, clean, soft, and powdery. It was a scent that reminded him of clean washing and of his childhood.

'Hi, Mum.'

'Hello again, Henry.'

'Look at this a moment.' He flipped the camera on his phone so she could see the view, then moved it around so she could see the surrounding gardens.

'Goodness, that's beautiful.'

'I know. You'd love it here.' He returned the camera to his face.

'I'm sure I would.' Her eyes shone as she smiled at him. 'But the best view is right in front of me now.'

'Ha! Thanks, Mum.' Henry resisted the urge to roll his eyes in embarrassment. 'You're always so kind.'

'You're my baby boy and I love seeing your handsome face. I miss you so much.'

'I miss you too, but you know you're welcome to come and stay anytime you like. I have the space.'

'I know, darling, and I'm grateful for the offer. I'm just—'

'Very busy there, I know, and you worry about Dad.'

His mum pursed her lips. 'I don't like to leave him to fend for himself.'

'I'm sure he'd manage. He's an adult, you know.' Henry swallowed down what he wanted to say next. His father was a grown man and he would cope perfectly well on his own, but he knew his mum was afraid he wouldn't. His father would then blame her, and she would face the fallout — his prolonged sulking, while denying he was upset, and it would go on for weeks.

'He needs me,' she breathed.

Henry gave a small dip of his head, not wanting to make his mum feel bad. His parents had been married a long time, and he knew they loved each other. His dad was a hard man though. Before retiring recently, he'd been a highly successful corporate lawyer. Bruce Clay valued ambition, self-discipline and a strong work ethic. Coming from a long line of lawyers, he'd had high expectations for his only son and Henry knew he'd found him disappointing. Hell, Henry had found himself disappointing, but he knew it stemmed from how his father saw him and it was hard sometimes to rise above that. When he'd been working in finance, his father had been proud, but now he was teaching, his father disapproved. Teaching was not the route to secure finances and career success, his father believed, and nothing else mattered.

'How've you been, Mum?' he asked, a note of tenderness in his voice.

She told him about the latest WI projects she'd been involved with as well as her work at the food bank and he listened, enjoying the sound of her voice and watching how her eyes lit up when she spoke about helping others. She was a kind woman, and he knew he hadn't always appreciated how compassionate she was when he was growing up. As a teenager, he'd seen her caring nature as a weakness at times, and occasionally told her as much, especially when she was trying to keep the peace between him and his father. Now, though, he saw exactly how strong she was and how her kindness was a strength few people possessed. He wished she'd be more selfish, but it wasn't in her nature and he knew she'd always put others, especially her husband and family, before herself. She'd worked as a counsellor for young carers for a while, and he knew she'd carried a lot of that with her for years. Seeing youngsters struggling to act like adults had often left her tearful and wishing she could do more. Feeling powerless to help others was the thing he'd once thought could be her undoing. But she endured, and she kept helping and she kept being there for her family.

'That all sounds great.' He smiled and her cheeks turned pink.

'Thanks, darling. So…' She licked her lips. 'Who was that lovely young woman at the café?'

'Her name is Rosa, and she owns the bookshop in the village.'

'A bookshop, eh? I'm sure you're spending lots of time there.' She laughed, aware that Henry had a serious book buying addiction.

'Some, it's true. You know me and my reading habit.'

'I do, my little bookworm, I do.' She winked at him. They shared a love for reading fiction. While he was growing up, they'd kept it secret from his father because Bruce only approved of non-fiction and educational books. 'But this Rosa … she's not your…'

His mum always did this, left pauses rather than asking full questions, and it made him shake his head. 'No. There's nothing between us.'

'Oh.' She raised her brows, then gave a small shrug. 'Never mind, darling. How's work?' She was proud of him for becoming a teacher even if his father wasn't. She had encouraged him to apply for the teacher training course when he'd told her how he felt about working in finance. She thought teaching was an admirable profession and said she was sure he would make a massive difference to the children he taught. Her faith in him and her encouragement had meant the world.

Henry told her about how well he'd settled in and how happy he was at the school and she smiled and nodded and asked questions about his colleagues and then things like if he was eating properly and getting enough rest.

'Well you look wonderful, Henry. The sea air is clearly doing you the world of good.'

'Thanks, Mum. How's Megan?'

Megan was his younger sister and the golden child of the family — at least in his father's eyes. She was a medical student, ambitious, and she'd shown a distinct lack of understanding of Henry's chosen career path. She often patronised him when they spoke so he limited phone calls to once a month with her, sometimes relying on a text instead to stay in touch, especially if she was on shifts. He felt bad about it from time to time, but justified it by telling himself she needed to rest and they could catch up later in the month. Megan had shown no interest in romance, and Henry wondered if seeing what he'd been through had affected her outlook in that respect. He loved Megan and thought she was incredible for choosing a medical career, but they were very different and so they'd often clashed over the years.

'Right then, Henry,' his mum said. 'I'd better get ready as I want to get dinner prepared before I go, so it's ready to pop in the oven when I get home.'

He bit back asking why his father couldn't do that and instead said, 'Have a great afternoon, Mum. Love you.'

'Love you too. Don't forget to stay in touch, now.'

'Never!' He blew her a kiss, then ended the call.

He put his phone away and gazed out at the view, watching the rhythmic push and pull of the sea and a pair of large, black cormorants gliding low over the waves. Down on the sand, a child, and a dog ran side by side chasing a ball and beyond that, a boat entered the harbour, its engine humming.

The village was bathed in morning sunshine now, and the amber and rust of the leaves on the trees was beautiful, the colours seeming brighter than ever before. It was as if he'd spent years wearing murky contact lenses, and day by day, his vision was clearing. The space from London and from his former life were helping him to move on, and it was in moments like this that he realised just how much he'd needed the change.

From now on, things could only get better…

8
ROSA

'Ooh! That muffin looks delicious!' Sita eyed the apple streusel muffin Rosa had ordered, along with a hot chocolate topped with marshmallows and whipped cream.

'Do you want a bite? Or I could get you one?' Rosa said.

'I probably shouldn't. I've already eaten a veggie sausage bap and a spiced pear croissant.' Sita giggled.

'Well, if you fancy one, you should have one. Or, just have a bite of mine.'

Sita shook her head. 'I'll resist for now, but next time I come here I'll have one.'

Rosa took a bite of the muffin and moaned. 'It's so good.'

Sita stood up and grabbed her purse from her bag. 'Sod it! I'm not resisting if they're that good. Want anything else?'

'I'm fine, thanks.'

Sita went to the counter of The Garden Café and Rosa sat back and took a sip of her hot chocolate. The café was one of her favourite places to eat in the village. She liked their seasonal menu and suspected it would be tremendously busy during the summer months when the village was flooded with tourists.

She had come to meet Sita for breakfast, but she was pleased to see Henry too. He'd looked so handsome this morning, and she'd been struck again by her visceral reaction to him, her heart racing with something she couldn't quite name. After swearing off men because of what had happened to her, she was pleasantly surprised by how attracted she was to Henry. She'd thought that after what she'd been through, she would never want to so much as look at another man, but with Henry it was different. There was just something about him she was drawn to: there was kindness in his eyes and his smile seemed so genuine. She couldn't help but like him.

'There!' Sita sat down and placed a plate on the table. 'If I hadn't ordered one of these muffins, I'd have thought about it all day, so it's better to satisfy the craving, I think.'

'Oh, I agree.' Rosa laughed. 'Enjoy!'

'Talking of enjoying…' Sita bit her muffin and closed her eyes. 'Deary me, that's delicious.' She chewed for a moment, holding up her hand to let Rosa know that she'd continue her point just as soon as she could. 'Talking of enjoying … I saw how Henry Clay looked at you and he was definitely enjoying the view.'

'What?' Rosa laughed and shook her head. 'I don't think so.'

'Oh he was, sweetie. Henry likes you. An idiot could spot it a mile away. The way he watched you so intensely when you spoke to him and his wistful expression when you invited him to join us…'

'How could you hear that?' Rosa frowned.

'Honey, I have three children. My ears are tuned in to a different frequency than most people's.'

Rosa giggled. Sita had always been funny and had an ability to make her laugh even when she was feeling blue.

'And if I'm not mistaken, having known you as long as I have, then I think you like him, too.'

Rosa was about to deny this, but Sita held her gaze, her big brown eyes fixed on Rosa's. Sita had known her a long time, since she was a child when she'd holidayed in Porthpenny with her aunt. She'd been crab fishing at the harbour one day when a small girl with black curly hair and big brown eyes had approached her and given her some tips on how to catch a crab. Sita had introduced herself and they'd become friends, and every time Rosa visited the Cornish village after that day, she'd always looked out for Sita. They'd spent many summer days splashing in the sea, sunbathing on the golden sand and chatting about life. Nothing had changed now they were adults. Sita was married with three boys but she was still the same bubbly, funny, caring person, and Rosa was delighted that she got to see more of her since her move. It was Sita who had encouraged Rosa to move here and set up her dream bookshop, and Rosa was incredibly grateful for her support.

Rosa sighed. 'He's very handsome, sweet and intelligent and he loves reading, but that's all there is to it. You know why I can't ever bring myself to date again. I just can't.' She bit her bottom lip as tears stung her eyes and Sita reached over the table and took her hand.

'I know you were hurt, and that's hard to overcome, but I also think you deserve someone who loves you in return.

Just because it went wrong before doesn't mean it will do again.'

Rosa blinked away her tears and met Sita's eyes. 'I know you mean well, but you don't understand because you've never been through what I have. I'm sorry … that sounds patronising. But you have Niels and he'd do anything for you. Rejection leaves a bitter taste in your mouth and so does…' She swallowed hard, not wanting to say the words and bring the betrayal into this moment with her friend. 'It's just hard to move on.'

'I know, darling. And I know I haven't been through what you have, but I did have my heart broken once … before Niels. There was a lad who came here for his summer holiday and I fell for his bright blue eyes and square jaw, his muscular build and surfing ability.' She grimaced. 'I spent several nights sneaking out of my parents' home and making out on the beach with him. Then his holiday came to an end, and we exchanged numbers, but I never heard from him again. I tried the number he'd given me and it was fake. A woman called Nigella answered and when I asked for him, thinking it must be his mother, she said she had no idea who I was taking about. I tried again, replacing one or two digits of the number he'd given me in case he'd made a mistake, but to no avail. The poohead had given me a fake number and so that was that. I never got to speak to him again.'

'I'm so sorry. You never told me about this before.'

Sita shrugged. 'I felt like such a fool. He'd strung me a few lines just to get into my knick — my good books…' She winked. 'And then after he got what he wanted, he left without so much as a backwards glance.'

'What a poohead.'

'Exactly.' Sita laughed. 'I was gutted at the time and blamed myself. If I'd been prettier, slimmer, funnier, known more about football … blah blah blah, then he'd have wanted to be with me. At the end of the day though, he was who he was and nothing was going to change that. Anyway…' She took another bite of muffin and chewed thoughtfully. 'I was on Facebook recently and he came up as a recommended friend because we have a mutual friend.'

'So you did what any self-respecting person would do and had a nose at his profile?'

'Of course I did!' Sita laughed. 'And what a lucky escape I had. Seems he's got fat and bald. He was handsome when he was younger in that sharp youthful way, but now…' She shuddered. 'Not that looks are everything, of course, but I think his meanness has emerged through his skin and now he looks mean too. Of course, he was a teenager back then and probably played the field a lot before he settled down. He's married now with children, well, teenagers by the look of it and he plays in a band.' She sniggered. 'There were some photos of him at gigs with what little hair he has left in a small ponytail — unless it's a stick-on one — and he was on stage acting like he was Rod Stewart.'

'Oh dear…'

'Exactly.' Sita nodded. 'I had a lucky escape. Just like you.'

'Things were further along for me though…' Rosa said.

'Of course they were. And I am so sorry for what you went through, my darling. So sorry. But … what I was trying to say to you is that we all get hurt at some point, but it doesn't mean we can't love again. Look at me and Niels.'

'You guys are the perfect match. I'm so glad you found him.'

'Well…' Sita sipped her latte. 'He kind of found me, didn't he?'

Niels had come to Porthpenny twelve years ago on a business trip and met Sita there. He fell deeply in love with her and proposed before the week was over. Niels had moved to Cornwall, and they'd married six months later and had three boys — Johan, ten, Daan, eight, and Willem, five. It was the perfect romance story and Rosa wished she could have the same, but for her things had been very different.

'Anyway … as I was saying, I think Henry likes you and you could do a lot worse than a sexy teacher.'

'I'll keep him as a friend, thank you very much.'

'We'll see!' Sita giggled. 'We will see. Trust me that Sita Vandermeer has a funny feeling about this. Something good is coming your way.'

'Hopefully it's another apple streusel muffin.' Rosa waggled her eyebrows, and Sita laughed hard.

'If all else fails, there's always cake, right?'

'Always.'

9

ROSA

*T*wo days later, Rosa had breakfast then showered and washed her hair. It was the day of the village harvest festival so she dressed warmly because even though it was sunny, the breeze coming in from the sea could be chilly. She put on jeans, boots, a black jumper, and a scarf with a book print she'd found online, then she added her down-filled jacket and a hat. She had never attended a village harvest festival, but Vinnie assured her of plentiful food, drink, music, and produce. It was how the local community celebrated the year they'd had, the crops they'd grown, as well as health and prosperity. Vinnie had added that by 'prosperity' he meant an attitude of gratitude because fortune could appear in many forms and not just financial wealth.

When she was ready, Rosa went down to the shop and checked the computer for any orders that had processed overnight. Then she made a coffee and drank it while gazing out of the window. This year, more than ever, she felt she had something to celebrate and to be thankful for. Her life had transformed in the past year, but she had much to be grateful for and so she would celebrate that today as a new member of the Cornish community.

She would go down to the harbour and the village square and join in with the festival, but first she had to collect someone. She'd spoken to Christopher the day before and asked if he intended on coming to the festival and he'd seemed hesitant, so she'd insisted that he join her. It wasn't far from his home but she didn't want the walk to tire him out so she'd drive him in then he could enjoy the festival. The more time she spent with him, the more she felt he was becoming like a grandfather, father, and friend all rolled into one. He was kind, caring and fascinating and she wanted to know more about him and his life. Anyone who lived into their nineties had a wealth of knowledge and experience to share, and she wanted him to feel that he was appreciated and cared about, just like any of her friends.

She drove to his home and when he opened the door, his face lit up. She was glad she'd made the effort to invite him and insisted on collecting him.

'Rosa!' he said, as if he hadn't been expecting her. 'Come on in.'

Bobby bounded towards her, so she crouched down and made a fuss of him while Christopher got his coat.

'Shall I put his coat on too?' she asked.

'That would be a marvellous help.' He handed her the dog's fleecy jacket, then the lead that she attached to his collar. 'Thank you again for this. I can't explain exactly how much I…' He trailed off, and she looked up from Bobby.

'Are you OK?'

He nodded, but he was covering his mouth with a hand, the fingers bumpy with arthritic lumps, the veins raised under the thin skin like the roots of a tree.

'I'm OK.' He gave a small cough. 'I'm just … an emotional old fool. Meeting you and having you care enough to come and get me … It's more than I deserve.'

'What? Don't say that, Christopher,' she said. 'Of course you deserve kindness and consideration. Doesn't everyone?'

'You, young lady, are an angel and I'm amazed someone who sees exactly how wonderful you are has not snapped you up.'

Rosa smiled but her stomach churned. If only it was that simple.

'Unless, of course, I'm being a fool and there's a story behind that fact that you're single.' He frowned. 'I know that these days we're not supposed to ask people if they're married and if they have children because it's not considered polite. In my day... well, we would have considered it a great shame for a beautiful young woman like you to be single. The children part … I understand well enough how tough that can be because, once again, in my day, everyone expected children to follow quickly if you got married. For my wife and I, that wasn't the case as you know, but for you … Is it OK if I ask you about those things? Please tell me if I'm overstepping the mark.'

Rosa smiled at him, then she went closer and opened her arms. 'Can I give you a hug?'

'I … I would like that very much.'

He opened his arms too and Rosa hugged him, pressed her face against the wool of his jacket and breathed in the smell of clean washing and cologne, of toast and shaving foam and the faint aroma of old house. Her eyes filled with tears as she thought about the years Christopher had been alive, the things he'd seen and done, the loss he'd suffered and the loneliness he must feel because of that loss. If you lived to your nineties, you'd see many friends and acquaintances pass away, see many changes in society and technology, see a very different world to when you were a child. Christopher had seen so much and it made her heart ache for him but also fill with joy because he had lived a long life that many would like to have.

When she stepped back, she saw his eyes were glistening, too, and she laughed softly.

'What is it?' he asked, pulling a handkerchief from his pocket and dabbing at his eyes.

'I was just thinking about how exceptional you are,' she said. 'Look at how smartly you're dressed and how sweet and kind you are. I feel privileged to know you.'

'Why young lady, the feeling is mutual. Rosa … that is the first hug I've had since my wife passed away.' His lower lip trembled, and Rosa felt her face crumple.

'That's so sad, Christopher.'

'Mayhap it is … but I also feel very grateful that you wanted to give me a hug.'

'Hugs are very important,' she said. 'They produce endorphins which boost our immune systems and our mood.'

'Well then, after that hug I shall surely live to see a hundred!' He chuckled.

'I hope so.' She looked down at Bobby. 'And the same goes for you, little man.'

Bobby barked and pawed at her leg.

Christopher locked his door while Rosa settled Bobby in the back of the van with his special harness then she helped Christopher to get comfortable.

'It's a beautiful day,' Christopher said as she drove them back to the shop.

'It is indeed. A beautiful day filled with possibilities.'

'Do you know what I haven't done in a long time?' he asked.

'What's that?'

'Crabbing.'

'Then that's what we'll do today,' she replied with a smile. 'Today we can do whatever you want, Christopher.'

'How wonderful.'

When she'd parked the van behind the shop, they got out and she set Bobby on the pavement, then handed his lead to Christopher. People already bustled through the village, making their way to the square and harbour where the stalls were set up. Aromas of hot dogs, onions, and roast chicken permeated the air, and she laughed as Bobby sniffed hard, his small head raised with interest.

'I think Bobby's hungry,' she said.

'Bobby is always hungry.' Christopher laughed. 'He has hollow legs.'

'Let's see what we can get him to fill them, shall we?'

Rosa took Christopher's arm, and they strolled down to the harbour with Bobby trotting along in front, nose in the air, small tail wagging with excitement. Rosa was glad she'd

made the effort to invite Christopher and that he'd appreciated the hug. The thought that he'd been without a hug in so
long made her sad and she hoped she was making a difference in his life. Kindness was free, and she thought people
should show it as often as they could do.

As well as embracing an attitude of gratitude … And right
now, Rosa was feeling very grateful indeed.

10

HENRY

*W*andering around the village harvest festival was a delight for the senses. It was a crisp, bright autumn Sunday and Henry was dressed warmly, aware that he would be outside for most of the day.

He stood in the village square and turned slowly, soaking up the sights, sounds, and smells. The salty tang of the sea lingered in the air, along with the earthy musk of cobblestones drying in the sun. Stretching away from the pretty coastal village were country lanes and rolling fields with patchwork meadows. Stone farmhouses and large barns dotted the landscape that was divided by hedgerows and bathed in shades of claret, ochre, orange and green. Further still, lay more villages and towns and if you kept going, as a crow flies, you'd reach the northern coast of Cornwall.

Stalls lined the pavements, brimming with local produce. Baskets of fat orange pumpkins, ruby-red apples, dark green cabbages, and potatoes of varying sizes sat on trestle tables. Scrumpy cider, elderflower cordial, ginger beer, and Cornish seaweed gin filled baskets on one stall. Another was selling baked goods: Cornish pasties with crimped edges and flaky golden pastry, fat shiny scones that looked irresistibly fluffy, clotted cream fudge with various additions like dark chocolate chips and rum and raisin, and apple turnovers stuffed with fresh white cream. His mouth watered as he gazed at the produce and pastries, the drinks, and treats.

People wandered around the stalls and the harbour dressed in waxed jackets, cosy knits, boots, and hats, carrying pumpkin spiced lattes, hot chocolates and mulled cider. Children queued for face painting, hot dogs, crepes and turns at crabbing and parents chatted to friends and neighbours, smiling and raising hands when they spotted Henry walking among them.

He stopped to buy a pasty and a coffee, then he walked down to the harbour and sat on a bench. The pastry was rich and buttery, the filling of meat, root veg, and potatoes savoury and satisfying. He washed the pasty down with the bitter coffee, its steam curling into the cool morning air, while watching as boats left the harbour, taking people on trips around the coastline. The boat engines hummed as they sliced through the glinting water and white wakes fanned out behind them like frothy lace.

Aware that there were activities taking place around the village today, he decided to make his way up to The Garden Café where he'd promised some of his pupils he would meet them and their parents to join their teams.

He dropped his rubbish in a bin, then walked along the path that led to the café. Music filled the air, and he gazed down at the beach where a choir had gathered to sing some traditional harvest hymns. The haunting beauty of the sea and cliffs stilled him; goosebumps erupted on his skin as he listened. This village, located here between the land and the sea, surrounded by endless sky, was the perfect place to be. He hadn't realised until he'd come here how much he needed this, how different he would feel when he was here and how it would help him unravel all the things that had weighed him down for so long.

Taking a few deep breaths of briny air, he turned and strode towards the café, a smile on his face and joy in his heart.

When he got there, a sight that would have been perfect in a movie greeted him. Bales of hay were arranged in circles with braziers at their centres, country music played from hidden speakers, aromas of wood smoke and barbecue drifted through the air, and piles of pumpkins sat in front of the café, ready for the carving competition.

'Sir!' He turned to see Johan Vandermeer running towards him. 'You came! Are you going to be on our team?'

Henry laughed. 'If that's what you want.'

Behind Johan, his mum, Sita, smiled and raised a hand in greeting. She had her five-year-old son Willem on her hip and he had his face buried in her neck.

'I'm so glad you came, Sir. I asked my mum to join our team, but Willem is being a cry-baby so she can't put him down.'

'What's wrong with Willem?' he asked, concern filling him.

'Nothing, really.' Johan rubbed a hand through his thick, black hair. 'He wanted to wear his superhero costume today, but Mum said it wouldn't be warm enough and he's been sulking since we left the house.'

'I'm sorry to hear that,' Henry said.

'It's OK, Sir,' Johan said. 'He'll get over it.' He gave a dismissive wave of his hand then pointed over at a table where people were queueing. 'Shall we sign up for the apple bobbing?'

'Apple bobbing?'

'Yes. It's lots of fun.'

'Sure.' Henry shrugged. 'I haven't bobbed for apples in a very long time though, so I could be awful.'

'You'll be great, Sir, I'm sure. Just remember to hold your breath so the water doesn't go up your nose.'

'Thanks for the tip.'

Henry stifled his laughter then followed Johan over to the stall and waited in line, listening to the boy's excited instructions about the best way to grab the apples with his mouth while avoiding drinking the water. It seemed like Johan had really thought about this and even got in some practice before the day.

11

ROSA

*R*osa had walked around the village with Christopher and made sure he had something to eat and drink. She'd tried to pay, but he'd insisted on treating her. They'd met up with Vinnie and he'd strolled around with them, chattering away about how much he was looking forward to the line dancing later on the beach.

'What would you like to do now?' she asked Christopher.

'Didn't you want to go up to The Garden Café?' he asked.

'I would like to head up there at some point, but it's a bit of a walk,' she said.

'I'm up for a walk,' he replied. 'It's the best exercise there is for an old man like me.'

'Are you sure?' She frowned. He was seemingly fit, but she worried that the incline on the way to the gardens would be hard on him. 'I could get the van and drive us up there?'

Christopher shook his head. 'The walk will be fine.'

'OK then. Shall we go there now?'

'Why not? As long as you don't mind walking a bit slower. Or you could go on ahead and I'll catch up with you?'

'No.' She shook her head. 'We'll go together.'

'I'm up for a wander,' Vinnie said.

They headed for the café, pausing a few times to watch the choir on the beach as they sang some traditional harvest hymns and then some pop favourites. It also gave Christopher the chance to have a rest without anyone drawing attention to the fact that this was what he was doing.

'It's like being in a movie,' Christopher said when they stopped the third time.

'I always think that when I'm walking and there's live music,' Vinnie said. 'It reminds me of scenes where characters go somewhere, and the music matches their mood. Like right now, it's a happy song so we can strut like John Travolta in *Saturday Night Fever*.' Vinnie demonstrated and Rosa and Christopher laughed at his exaggerated movements.

'Can you perform his dance moves, though?' Christopher asked.

'The disco ones?' Vinnie replied.

'Those.' Christopher nodded.

'I think so. I'll have to practise first, though.' Vinnie winked at them.

'I love that movie,' Christopher said wistfully. 'Dolly and I saw it when it first came out, and it was so much fun. The soundtrack is fantastic.'

Rosa smiled as Christopher talked about the movie and his favourite songs from the soundtrack. Whenever he spoke about Dolly and their happy times, it lit him up and he seemed years younger than he was. He had lived such a long time and yet she got the impression from what he said that time had flown past and ninety-two years was nothing at all. She'd only lived for thirty-five years and that had gone quickly, but she couldn't imagine getting to her nineties.

'And here we are.' Christopher paused in front of the café gardens and Bobby sat down and gazed up at his owner. 'Just … catch my breath a moment.' His hand moved to sit over his ribs and Rosa tried not to stare as he breathed slowly in and out, his lips tight with the strain. She'd thought it might be too much for him, but he had insisted and she didn't feel she had any right to tell him what he should or shouldn't do. He was a proud man and there was a certain amount of defiance in how he'd walked up here without so much as a cane, so he deserved to be admired and not patronised.

'Of course.' Rosa stood next to him and watched Vinnie, who'd decided to try out his disco moves.

'I can do this one,' Vinnie said as he threw one arm in the air and the other behind him, then sang in a high voice that she suspected was meant to imitate the Bee Gees. He swapped arms a few times, then wiggled his hips and pouted at them and Rosa and Christopher giggled.

'Oh my goodness, Vinnie, you're mad!' Rosa said.

'Actually, I think he's got it perfectly.' Christopher smiled. 'I thought he was John Travolta there for a minute.'

'I'll take that!' Vinnie gave a small bow, then opened the gate to the café gardens. 'After you.'

Rosa and Christopher walked through the gate, and Bobby and Vinnie followed. The gardens were busy, and she scanned the people, searching for familiar faces. Music played from speakers and the sound of people talking and laughing greeted them along with aromas of roasting meat and vegetables.

'Let's find a seat, then we can get some drinks,' she said.

They wandered through the gardens and found a spare circle of hay bales with a brazier in the middle. She helped Christopher to sit down on one, then handed him the rug from the side of it to put over his knees. 'Just in case you get cold after the exertion of the walk,' she said. Bobby jumped up next to Christopher and looked around him.

'Thank you, Rosa. I'm very cosy now,' he said.

'No problem. I'll get us a drink. Do you want anything to eat?'

'Not yet, dear, as I'm still full from earlier, but maybe later.'

She turned to Vinnie. 'What do you want?'

'Whatever you have,' he said.

'Stay with Christopher and Bobby then and I won't be long.'

She walked towards the café, but shouting and cheering from the gardens to the side of the building caught her attention, so she went in that direction to see what was going on.

On the grass were two large bowls and people were kneeling in front of the bowls with their hands laced behind their backs. Around them, people shouted and cheered words of encouragement.

As she watched, the person closest to her raised his head and turned to drop an apple into another bowl. They were bobbing for apples! She hadn't played this game in years.

When the man ducked his head again, then emerged with another apple, she realised it was Henry and next to him was another teacher from the school.

Henry dropped another apple in the bowl and then a whistle sounded and Pearl waved her hands in the air. 'Time's up! Well done to both teams. Now, while Ellie changes the water and gets more apples for the next round, I'll count the apples.'

Henry waited, wiping his face with a towel while Pearl counted the apples in his bowl and then the other man's. She made a note on a pad, then went to Henry and took his hand before raising it above his head. 'And our winner of Round 2 is Mr Clay!'

Applause filled the air and Henry grinned at everyone, then Johan Vandermeer appeared and high-fived Henry. 'Well done, Sir! I knew you could do it!'

'Thanks, Johan.' Henry smiled. 'Your turn next?'

'Yes, sir!' Johan rolled his shoulders and flexed his hands as he prepared for his turn.

Henry turned then and looked directly at Rosa. She felt like she'd been snooping and glanced away, but when she looked back at him, he was smiling.

'Hello.' He joined her at the periphery of the crowd.

'Hi.' She smiled. 'You looked like you enjoyed that.'

'It's more fun than I remembered,' he said. 'Even if I got wet.'

He was still holding the towel, and he rubbed it over his face and neck.

'Would you like a drink?' she asked. 'I was just going to get one for myself, Christopher and Vinnie.' She gestured behind her and Henry looked over that way.

'Uhm … I wouldn't mind something warm.'

'Coffee?'

'That would be great, thanks. I would offer to help you, but I know Johan wants me here to cheer him on.'

'That's fine. I'll bring it out for you.'

'That's very kind.' His smile made her stomach flutter and a gentle heat filled her cheeks.

'I won't be long,' she said, then she forced her feet to move. Standing there staring at him, even if he did look gorgeous with those blue-green eyes and his auburn hair damp around the front from bobbing for apples, was still rude.

What surprised her even more was that she'd been tempted to take the towel to catch the water droplets he'd missed on his right temple and lean in close to see if he smelt as good as he looked. To find out if his skin was warm or cold and if he would press a gentle kiss to her cheek in the way she could imagine him doing.

What was wrong with her? She'd decided long ago that men were not on her agenda and yet here she was, lusting after Henry Clay. He was probably just like her ex and if she got close to him, he'd hurt her and she didn't think that she'd be able to pull herself together again. Surely one person's heart could only take so much? This village was her new beginning. She couldn't allow any man to ruin that for her, could she? Or would Henry Clay simply make everything even better?

ROSA

*R*osa returned with a tray of drinks to find Henry cheering for Johan as he bobbed for apples then clapping when he won.

'Here you go,' Rosa said, and Henry accepted a mug of coffee.

'Thank you.'

'So you won?' she asked.

'We did, but it was all down to Johan and the rest of the team.'

Johan ran over and jumped up and down with excitement. 'We won, Sir, and it's all because of you! Mr Clay is amazing, Rosa.'

She smiled at her friend's eldest son, and he beamed back.

Henry held up a hand and Johan gave him a high five, then he ran back to his mum and dad who were talking to Pearl.

'He's a great lad,' Henry said. 'All three of the brothers are polite and diligent.'

'Sita and Niels are good parents.' She looked over at her friend surrounded by her husband and three sons, and her heart squeezed with love and admiration. 'Sita's one of my oldest friends.'

'She's lucky to have you,' he said, holding her gaze. 'From what I've seen, you're kind, sweet, and caring.'

Rosa opened her mouth to reply, but her mind had gone blank. Was he being genuine? She wished she didn't have to question people's motives now, but it was hard not to. Trusting was difficult when she'd been so badly betrayed.

'I mean, few people would be so kind to an elderly gent.' He nodded over at Christopher, who was smiling at something Vinnie had said to him.

'He's a lovely man,' she said. 'I can't bear the thought of him being lonely. He's such a great age, and he deserves to have company and people around who care about him.'

'I agree.' Henry sipped his coffee. 'Do you need a hand with that tray?'

'Oh...' She'd forgotten she was holding it. 'No, it's fine. I should take their drinks over.'

'Are you staying for a while?' he asked.

'I expect so.'

'There's pumpkin carving next.' He waggled his brows, and she laughed. 'Fancy being on my team.'

'Goodness, I don't think I'd be very good at that. Can I just watch?'

'Of course. But, you know, if you want to cheer me on ... I'd like that.'

'I will. I promise.'

'Brilliant.'

They stood gazing into each other's eyes, the space between them charged with something as yet unsaid, the air filled with electricity. Warmth spread through Rosa's chest. Her skin prickled with the awareness of his proximity and her fingers twitched as if they might reach for him. But then Johan came over again and tapped Henry's arm, snapping them out of the trance they seemed to have fallen into. 'Sir? Are you ready for another round?'

'More bobbing for apples?' Henry's eyes widened as if he was trying to bring himself back to reality.

'Yes. Best of three rounds, Pearl said.'

'Cool.' Henry flashed a grimace at Rosa, but then he turned and said to Johan, 'Be there in a minute.'

'Looks like you're not out of the water yet,' Rosa said and Henry snorted.

'I see what you did there.'

'I guess I'll see you later then,' she said.

'I can't wait,' he whispered as she walked away, and the words sent a delightful shiver down her spine.

Something was happening here, and she wasn't sure if it was real or just the magic of autumn in the air at The Cornish Garden Café. If only she could trust herself enough to find out…

Back with Christopher and Vinnie, she handed them their drinks, then sat next to Christopher. The temperature had dropped as the afternoon wore on and Christopher said, 'Come under this rug a bit, dear. No sense being cold.'

'Thanks.' She slid it over her legs and cupped her mug between both hands.

'What's going on between you and Mr Teacher?' Vinnie asked, making her splutter coffee.

'I was going to ask the same thing.' Christopher tilted his head.

She fumbled to set her mug down without spilling her coffee, avoiding their enquiring eyes. 'What? Nothing.'

'Doesn't seem that way to me.' Vinnie cocked a dark brow. 'From where I'm sitting, it looked like there's a spark between you.'

'Same.' Christopher nodded.

'Behave yourselves.' She tried not to smile. 'We're just friends.'

'Sure and I'm actually John Travolta,' Vinnie said, rolling his eyes. 'Henry likes you and you like him. Why don't you save yourselves some time and get on with it?'

'Vinnie … it's not that simple,' she said and her cheeks flushed as Christopher and Vinnie stared at her. 'Please don't ask me to elaborate because I don't want to talk about it right now. Just … things aren't straightforward for me. I can't be frivolous about love and lust and … all that stuff.'

Christopher reached out and rubbed her arm, and she smiled at him.

'I'm OK. I just … I have reasons for not wanting to get involved with anyone again.'

'One life though, Rosa. And you're a catch, you know? I get that you've been hurt, but you get one life and you should live it, girl.' Vinnie held her gaze with such intensity that her eyes burned. 'I'm not dismissing what you've been through just saying that not all men are bad. Look at me and Christopher.'

Christopher laughed. 'It's true, Rosa. If you pick the right man, he will cherish you until the day he dies.'

'Oh…' Her vision blurred so she dabbed at her eyes with a tissue. 'Please don't say such nice things.'

'You deserve to be treasured, Rosa.' Christopher took her hand and raised it, then pressed a gentle kiss to her skin. 'I feel like you're my adopted granddaughter and I would like to see you happy if it's the last thing I do see.'

'Stop now!' A tear escaped her right eye and ran down her cheek and Christopher gently wiped it away with a gnarled finger.

'Why don't you invite him down to the line dancing at the beach later?' Vinnie asked. 'Give you a chance to get hot and sweaty with him without the risk of … you know… other pursuits that would also get you hot and sweaty.'

'Vinnie!' Rosa glanced at Christopher.

'It's OK, Rosa. I have lived, you know. You don't need to avoid sex talk for my benefit.' Christopher chuckled.

'Oh my god, what am I going to do with you two?' Rosa picked up her coffee again and drained it then set it on the tray. 'I get what you're saying, that life is short and not all men are the same and I promise I will think about your points. But let me take some time to gather my thoughts and to process how I'm feeling because it's hard to trust my gut these days.'

'You can trust your gut, though.' Christopher nodded. 'Whatever happened to you before ... I'm sure you had a feeling that something wasn't right.'

She sighed and rubbed at her eyes. 'I did, but I didn't know what. I wanted everything to be OK and so I didn't listen to my gut instinct.'

'And what is that same gut instinct telling you about Henry?' he asked.

Rosa looked over at Henry, where he was standing with Johan and his family waiting for the next round to begin. He was talking and laughing and seemed to glow with an easy happiness at being a part of the community. Henry had been nothing but nice to her and to others, and she did have a good feeling about him. There was no edge to him, nothing to suggest that he could change at the flip of a switch or that he had any ulterior motives. He'd recently moved to the village to start a new life there, so just like her, he wanted to be happy and settled. There would, no doubt, be reasons he'd moved to Cornwall and one day, perhaps he'd share them with her. Could she share her past with him? Was she brave enough?

Perhaps...

But for now she would enjoy the afternoon and consider asking him to the line dancing at the beach later on. After all, there was no harm in dancing with him, was there? And it might just get Vinnie and Christopher off her back for a bit.

Turning back to them, she smiled because she knew that they only had her best interests at heart, and she wanted to give them something back for caring. These two men who were quickly becoming her found family as she started her new life.

13

HENRY

*A*fter bobbing for apples, Henry went inside the café to warm up a bit. In the toilets, he put his head under the drier to dry his hair and face, then he looked at himself in the mirror and laughed. His hair stuck up like he'd been shocked, and his face was bright red from the heat. He pushed his hands through his hair to tidy it as best he could, then he went back outside.

Rosa was sitting with Christopher and Vinnie and she looked contented, like a woman sitting with her grandpa and brother. They could have been family, and it made him wonder about her and if she had an actual family to turn to. If not, how did she manage? Henry had his parents, sister and friends too. Not having family would be hard, he suspected. Despite his difficult relationship with his father and his father's frequent disappointment in him, Henry knew his father would be there for him. His mother and sister would be there no matter what, he was certain of that, and his mum always made him feel safe and loved. Did Rosa have that security, or was she alone in the world?

Something fluttered in his chest and he rubbed a hand there as he wondered at it. He barely knew Rosa, and yet he felt like there was a connection growing between them. He'd felt this once before and it hadn't worked out and it had terrified him. But this time, he was older and wiser, and not being influenced by what others around him wanted. He was an adult now, and he was more certain about who he was. He escaped his father's expectations, a loathed job, and an unhappy relationship by moving to another part of the country. To him, it was a step toward self-discovery. The relationship he'd left had been wrong on so many levels, but he was in a position now to create a more equal partnership with the right woman. Previously, he'd been unable to devote himself fully because he wasn't being true to himself. He was living a life that others wanted for him and not the life he wanted for himself. Now, the time had arrived for him to choose, to embrace love, and to develop as a person.

A woman like Rosa could be the perfect partner for him if she felt the same. There was something else, though — something deeper inside him that stirred whenever he thought about her. It wasn't easy to admit, and others might baulk at it, but it was there, undeniable. He wanted to be there for her, to protect her. Not out of weakness or necessity, but out of a quiet, instinctive need. Rosa was clearly a strong and independent woman, but even the strongest people needed someone by their side. And maybe — just maybe — he could be that someone for her.

'Mr Clay?' A hand tugged at his arm, and he turned to find Johan grinning at him.

'Yes, Johan?'

'Can we carve pumpkins now?'

He laughed. 'Yes, of course.' Looking back over at Rosa he waved and caught her eye. She nodded, then said something to her companions before getting up and coming to him.

'Yes?'

'It's time for pumpkin carving now. Would you like a go?'

'Oh…' She pulled a face. 'My hands are a bit cold, to be honest. Could I just watch you instead?'

'Only if you cheer him on,' Johan said with a cheeky grin.

'I can do that.' Rosa nodded.

'Come on, then.' Johan led them over to a table where Pearl was standing with Jasper Holmes. His partner, Ellie, was there too, along with his two children, Mabel and Alfie.

'Right then … first up we have Jasper versus Henry.' Pearl ticked off their names on the list on her notepad.

'Go on, Daddy! You can do it!' Alfie said, his little face filled with determination. 'Do the punkin face we planned.'

'Punkin?' Johan's eyes widened.

'It's OK,' Rosa whispered. 'Pumpkin can be hard to pronounce.'

'OK.' Johan shrugged. 'I understand that because my brother Willem, who's also five, can't say hippopotamus or elephant.'

'What does he say instead?' Henry asked.

'Hitopotamoose and hephalant.' Johan laughed.

'Wow! Two new creatures right there.' Rosa winked. 'The tale of the hitopotamoose and the hephalant.'

Henry took a seat at the table next to Jasper. They shook hands and swished each other luck.

'Three. Two. One. Go!' Pearl clapped her hands and Henry took a deep breath then got to work. He'd thought about what he could do to the pumpkin, but in reality, it was much tougher than he'd imagined. Meanwhile, to his left, Jasper appeared to know what he was doing and to be doing it quickly. Nearby, Ellie and Jasper's children cheered him on and a crowd gathered around them all. A bead of sweat ran down Henry's forehead and he shook his head but couldn't move it. Suddenly, a gentle hand pressed a tissue there and he looked up to find Rosa smiling down at him.

'Thanks.' He flashed her a smile.

'No problem. You need to be able to see what you're doing.'

'And I couldn't use these…' He looked down at his sticky orange hands and grimaced.

As he worked, Pearl called out how long they had left and he tried to focus. The pumpkin evolved a shape as he tried to carve it to look the way it did in his mind.

'Go on, Daddy, do that punkin right!' Alfie shouted.

Henry looked over at Johan and saw that the boy was cheering him on, but in that moment he knew that even if his carving skills were better than Jasper's, he couldn't win this. Alfie needed his daddy to win, so that was what would happen. Losing didn't have to be a bad thing at all and all children needed to learn that at some point. But he suspected Alfie was more emotionally invested in this than Johan anyway, and so he slowed down, held the pumpkin out to look at his handiwork, then tweaked it a bit.

'And that's it, guys! Time is up!' Pearl said loudly and they downed tools and sat back to wait.

'Wow! Love what you did there.' Jasper admired Henry's pumpkin.

'Yeah but yours is outstanding,' Henry said, filled with admiration.

'If the judges can now score the work, please,' Pearl said, and a few locals walked over to the table and assessed the pumpkins while Henry and Jasper went to wash their hands.

When they came back, Pearl was smiling at them.

'So, as you know, the winner will get a voucher to bring their family to the café to eat a meal for free. The judges have decided unanimously that the winner is…'

'Daddy!' Alfie said and everyone laughed.

'Yes, indeed. You're right, Alfie. Your daddy is the winner.'

Alfie ran to Jasper, and he scooped him up and hugged him tight. Henry clapped his hands while trying to swallow the lump in his throat. Alfie's delight at his daddy's win was clear, and the love between them was very moving to see. Mabel also ran to Jasper, and he hugged her too, and then Ellie joined them. They were a beautiful little family unit, demonstrating once again, Henry thought, that family didn't have to be all about blood but about love and compassion, kindness, and support. Ellie wasn't the children's biological mother, but she loved them nonetheless.

Henry had once felt pressure to start a family and that others had mapped out his life without his consent. It had made him think that having children wasn't something he'd ever want or need. Seeing this display of love and solidarity though, now there was no pressure on him, he felt differently. Perhaps one day he would want a family, would want to have children and to be a dad. If he ever got the chance to do that, he would take the best of what his father had done for him and forget the worst, then be the dad he would want for himself and for his children. He would be like Jasper and do everything with his children at the forefront of his mind, be the very best dad he could be and make them proud of him.

He felt like he was being watched, so he turned and found Rosa gazing at him. Something in her eyes made his chest tight, and he struggled to suck in a breath. He saw her dilated pupils and slightly parted lips, realised she was experiencing something too. Had she understood what he was seeing? What he was feeling? What he was thinking? Was it possible that they had a connection strong enough to build into something more?

He was about to go over to her when he saw Vinnie come to her side and whisper something in her ear. Her expression changed, and she turned and crossed the gardens with him and the moment was gone. Johan came to Henry and told him he really liked the shape of a fish that he'd carved into the pumpkin but if he'd been a bit more skilled, he could have carved something like Jasper had done — a mini pumpkin inside the mouth of the bigger pumpkin. Henry simply nodded and agreed because he didn't have the heart to tell Johan that he hadn't carved a fish. It was, in fact, a cat — so it seemed his carving skills definitely weren't up to scratch after all…

1 4

ROSA

*R*osa hurried back to Christopher with Vinnie, and she crouched in front of him.

'Are you OK?' she asked.

Christopher had gone very pale and his lips were tight, as if he was in pain.

'I am absolutely fine,' he said. 'Just a bit tired. I've had a lot of fresh air today.'

'You have. Do you want us to take you home now?' she asked.

He looked at her and at Vinnie. 'I don't want to go home at all, but … well, perhaps I need to have a nap. Dammed ageing.' He sighed and rolled his eyes. 'The mind is willing, but the body isn't always up to it.'

'Nothing to do with age,' Vinnie said. 'I love an afternoon nap and often need one. If I grab forty winks, I'm as good as new. How about if we take you back and I'll stay with you while you nap, then bring you back out?'

'Oh young man, I couldn't ask that of you.' Christopher shook his head.

'I'll come with you,' Rosa said.

'Oh no.' Vinnie tutted. 'You need to ask that dashing dude to the line dancing. Chris … You don't mind me calling you Chris, do you? It's just Christopher is such a mouthful … So, Rosa, Chris and I will be just fine. In fact, I'll come home with you and have a wee snooze myself in the chair while you nap, then we can go to the beach for the dancing and drinks later on.'

'Only if you're sure?' Christopher said.

'I'm sure, Chris…' Vinnie shook his head. 'Nope. I have to call you Christopher because you don't look like a Chris.'

'That's fine. Call me whatever you like.' Christopher chuckled as he stood up and Bobby jumped down off the hay bale.

'Shall I get the van?' Rosa asked, concern making her shoulders tight. Poor Christopher looked exhausted.

'No, no. I'll walk slowly home.' Christopher accepted Vinnie's arm though, and Vinnie took Bobby's lead in his other hand. 'Thank you both. I've had a wonderful day.'

'It's not over yet.' Rosa gave him a hug. 'We'll have more fun this evening.'

'I sincerely hope so, dear.'

'I have to know you're OK, so I'll walk with you and then I'll come back here. I can't let you two go alone.'

She took Christopher's other arm, and they left the café gardens together. Three friends. Three people who cared about one another, along with a funny little dog they all adored.

*A*lmost an hour later, Rosa was on her way to the café gardens when she saw a crowd of people heading down to the beach. It seemed she'd missed the rest of the pumpkin carving and now the focus had turned to the dancing. She didn't mind because she'd helped Vinnie get Christopher settled and then she'd made them both a cup of tea and stayed to drink a cup, too. Once Christopher had dozed off on the sofa, she tidied up a bit, then left Vinnie to it. He'd been nodding off himself in one of Christopher's large armchairs as the TV screen had flickered with an antiques programme, the volume down low. Bobby had curled up in his basket in front of the fireplace where a fire flickered, keeping them cosy all as the afternoon grew darker and the lamps glowed in the corners of the room.

Now, strolling towards the beach, she shivered as the bracing breeze coming in off the sea wrapped itself around her. On the beach, fires glowed in portable fire pits; near the cliffs, someone had erected a stage, illuminated by string lights and a spotlight that lit up the center of the stage. It seemed like everyone from the village had come down to the beach and she could hear people talking, singing, and the rhythmic caress of the sea as it lapped at the shore like it was keen to join in with the harvest festival.

In front of the stage, a makeshift dancefloor had been crafted from pallets topped with wooden planks. A band was setting up on the stage, testing the sound system with bursts of static and tuning instruments, and she realised they were getting ready for the line dancing. She'd never done it before and worried she'd be a complete failure at it, coordination not being her strong suit at all, but if she didn't try, she'd never know. She'd watched others do it on YouTube videos and they looked like they were having fun, so she would try to relax and just enjoy herself. One life and all that, as Vinnie and Christopher liked to keep reminding her. Vinnie would be a king on the dancefloor anyway, so hopefully some of his confidence would rub off on her.

Realising she was thirsty, she looked for the refreshments stand and saw that it was just up from the sand on the way to the harbour, so she went to get a drink. When she had a cup of mulled cider, she carried it down to the beach and sat on the sand, watching as the small waves rolled in. As the sun sank in the sky, coral and amethyst hues bathed the horizon in a quiet symphony of colour, and the sea glowed silvery-purple, as if someone had substituted the water with liquid silver that shimmered in the dim light.

She sipped her cider, and emotion welled inside her, taking her by surprise. She wasn't sad, but she was emotional because the sight before her was breathtaking and because she'd had such a wonderful day. Her life hadn't worked out the way she'd thought it would, but that was OK because there was so much to be grateful for now. The journey that had brought her to this point had taught her a lot and left her with scars, but that was real life. No one got away completely unscathed, and no one had all the answers. She was still learning and she would be for as long as she lived, but that was all right too. She was willing and able to keep learning and she would do so gladly — learning about herself and about others and about all the beauty there was to be found in the world. Life had taught her it was easy to find the sadness and the darkness, but far better to look for the light because that was where the beauty, the joy, and the love resided.

Hearing her name, she looked up to see Henry walking towards her, so she dried her eyes and stood up, dusting the sand from the back of her jeans. In the glow of the setting sun, he was enchanting, his handsome face the most beautiful thing she'd ever seen. In that moment, she knew she wanted to give things a chance with him. She wanted to get to know him better, to find out how he felt about her and to see if there was something special growing between them. For a long time, she'd shut herself off from the possibility of finding love again, but Henry was different. Henry was special. Who knew, perhaps Henry was *the one*.

Her one.

Her person.

Perhaps…

15

HENRY

*A*s Henry reached Rosa, the band announced the imminent start of the line dancing. His stomach flipped over. He hadn't line danced in years, not since he was a teenager, but he wanted to try again, especially if it gave him a chance to dance close to Rosa.

'You coming?' he asked.

She looked behind him. 'I haven't seen Christopher and Vinnie yet. Did you pass them on your way here?'

He shook his head. 'No, but it was busy so they could be on the way or perhaps they've stopped in the village for something to eat or drink.'

'They could have.' She checked her phone but held it up to show him there were no messages.

'Do you want to look for them?' he asked.

'No, it's fine. I'm sure they'll come down when they're ready. They could still be sleeping.'

'Went for a nap, did they?'

'Christopher was exhausted and I think Vinnie was grateful for the excuse to grab forty winks himself.'

Henry laughed. 'Nothing like an afternoon nap.'

She gestured at the dancefloor where people were gathering. 'Shall we go over?'

'Sure.'

When they got there, two women were handing out cowboy hats, so they accepted one each.

'I'm not sure about the colour.' Henry eyed the bright blue of the hat he'd been given.

'It's not very authentic looking, is it?' She giggled as she placed the emerald green hat on her head.

'It suits you, though.' He smiled because she looked good with the hat on top of her long white-blonde hair. 'Shall we take our jackets off?' he asked, realising they'd likely get warm.

'Good idea.' She removed hers and handed it to him, then he took them over to a rock where others were leaving their coats and set them on top of the pile.

'Right then. Here we go.' He flashed her a wink, and then they stood waiting while everyone lined up.

She looked up at him; excitement and uncertainty filling her eyes, as if she wanted to look forward to this but feared fully letting go.

'Hey…' He held out his hand. 'It will be fun. I promise.'

She looked at his hand, then entwined her fingers with his. 'What if I make a fool of myself?'

'We can make fools of ourselves together, so don't worry at all.' He squeezed her hand, and she squeezed back.

The band started to play a familiar country song, and a woman strode onto the stage, then waved at the crowd. 'Hey y'all! Are you ready?'

'We are!' everyone chorused back.

'Well come along then. Let's get dancing!'

She led them through the moves: clap, stomp, turn, and back. They practised it a few times and then once they'd got the hang of it; they got going for real. Henry lost his rhythm a few times and went the wrong way, which made Rosa giggle. He bumped into her and a few other people several times when he wobbled, but he eventually found his rhythm and Rosa found hers. She was a natural and he couldn't help watching how she swung her hips and relaxed into the music, how she stomped her feet with determination and clapped with gusto.

Soon, they were dancing in tune with the music, the crowd, and each other. Their hands brushed together a few times and each time, he got a jolt of electricity up his arm. Whenever their eyes met, a similar jolt passed between them, fusing them physically and emotionally, igniting sparks like mini-fireworks.

As the music sped up, so did the dancing, and soon they were whirling around on the dancefloor, the wooden boards bouncing beneath their feet, the cheers of the dancers filling the evening and their breath emerging like puffs of smoke into the cold air.

There was just the sky above them, the pulse of the beat, and their warm bodies, and they danced like the weight of the past had lifted — if only for the time of the dance.

When the music ended, Henry took Rosa's hand, and they stood facing each other: breathless, chests heaving, grinning like they'd just learnt how to be happy for the first time.

'Wow!' she said eventually, her fingers still entwined with his. 'That was really something.'

'You were amazing.'

'I wasn't as bad as I thought I'd be, but I don't know about amazing.'

'Believe me, you were.' He stepped closer to her, so close their fronts nearly touched and he gently stroked her cheek with the pad of his thumb. He almost leant forwards to kiss her, then he realised what he was doing and where he was. As a teacher in the village, it wasn't a good idea to kiss Rosa in public, and so he sighed inwardly and stepped back a bit. Besides which, perhaps Rosa didn't want to be kissed, and he was merely following his instincts and not thinking about her feelings.

But when he met her eyes again, she was smiling, and she placed a hand on his chest right over his heart.

She blinked, her lashes framing her beautiful amber eyes. 'That was really something.'

'The dancing?' he asked, his voice gruff with longing.

'And what almost happened then...' She let out a small nervous laugh, then she licked her lips. 'Are you thirsty?'

'I could use a drink.'

'Shall we go and get one?'

'Good plan. I'll grab our jackets because we'll feel the cold now.'

When he joined her again, he helped her into her jacket then she took his hand again. They walked back along the beach and up to the refreshments stand, holding hands as if they did this every day.

And right then, it felt natural to Henry. As if his hand should always have been holding hers.

16

ROSA

*A*cross the beach, the fire pits flickered, their red-orange glow painting dancing shadows on the sand, the logs crackling and sending showers of copper sparks into the night sky. Stars, like diamond dust scattered across a never-ending indigo canvas, twinkled above. The moon cast its silvery light on the dark, undulating sea, creating a shimmering pathway to the distant, hazy horizon. The salty tang of the sea air mingled with the wood smoke — a warm, comforting scent.

Most of the villagers had gone home now or made their way to one of the village pubs, but Rosa and Henry remained, sitting on a log that smelt of seaweed and smoke, while opposite them Christopher sat in a camping chair that Henry had found for him with Bobby at his feet. Vinnie was reclining on a picnic blanket on the sand. They all nursed cups of mulled cider and were relaxed and sated after a supper of fish and chips smothered in salt and vinegar that they'd eaten from the paper. It had been a wonderful day and Rosa had enjoyed herself; now she was sleepy and contented.

'I have had the best time,' Christopher said. 'I'm very grateful to you three for involving me in your day.' His voice wobbled and Rosa sat forwards.

'Christopher, there's no need to thank us. We're friends and friends involve one another in things.'

'It's been some time since I've been involved in anything. It's my fault, I know. After I lost Dolly, I shut myself away. I couldn't bear to think that life could go on without her. I felt guilty for living, if that makes sense. Guilty that I was still here when she was gone. How could I get up every day, wash, eat and drink, walk in the fresh air when my beautiful girl was in the ground?'

'Oh Christopher…' Rosa shook her head. 'It must be so hard.'

'It is terrible and yet … I know she would want me to keep going. I always said to her that after I was gone from this world, she was to keep living and to make the most of every day. She was to enjoy herself for as long as she could because I couldn't bear to know that she wasn't happy.' He rubbed his chest. 'I wanted her to live. I always wanted to go first because I told her the thought of living without her was too awful to bear.'

'That's understandable,' Henry said. 'When you find the one, you don't want to be without them.' He glanced at Rosa and her breath caught in her throat.

'Exactly that.' Christopher gave a small nod. 'Being without Dolly is painful. I miss her so much it's a physical pain. But I can also hear her telling me I'd better not waste a day of life being sad because time waits for no one and I'll be joining her soon enough.' He reached down and patted Bobby's head and the dog peered up at him, love and devotion in his dark eyes. 'After I lost her … I shut myself away and lay in bed, wanting to give up, but then this little chap came and licked my face, my hands, my feet, and I knew I had to get up for his sake. I couldn't lie there while he was hungry, thirsty, or in need of a visit to the garden. And so I got up, and I went about my day. I was like a zombie...' He sighed. 'But I did it. Then I did the same the next day and the day after that and soon a week had passed. I got through the next two weeks and the funeral and then six months had gone by. Now it's been two years, and that seems incredible. How have my arms not held my Dolly for two whole years?'

They all fell silent as they contemplated Christopher's question. His loneliness was palpable and Rosa wished she could help him heal his heart, but she also knew that while she could be there for him, she could never bring his Dolly back.

'I decided when that thought hit me that it was time to clear the house,' Christopher continued. 'I went to the bookshop and met Rosa and now ... I can hardly believe it, but I have three new friends. It's almost like Dolly sent you to me so I could enjoy my final days.'

'What do you mean final days?' Vinnie's voice rose, and he placed a hand on Christopher's knee.

'Just a figure of speech, lad.' Christopher smiled. 'I meant it as in ... I know I don't have long left but now I have friends who have encouraged me to attend the harvest festival and to eat, drink and be merry. And I have had a blast. Honestly ... It means the world to me. You've been so kind looking out for me today and recently and I feel happy. It's been a long time since I could say that. Thank you from the bottom of my heart.' He placed a hand over his heart, and Rosa's eyes stung. She felt like she would start sobbing at any moment, so when Henry reached over and took her hand, she flashed him a grateful smile.

'It's a pleasure, Christopher,' Henry said. 'We're grateful for your friendship too.'

'What do I have to offer?'

'More than you know,' Rosa said. 'You're kind, funny and we love listening to your stories about your life and what Porthpenny was like in years gone by.'

'It's fascinating.' Henry nodded. 'Plus, Rosa and I are relatively new to the village and so we're delighted to have made friends with you, too. It works both ways.'

'Anyone for another drink?' Vinnie asked, then he stifled a yawn.

'I think I should probably head home soon,' Christopher said as he finished his cider. 'I'm rather tired and I think Bobby is too.'

'I'll walk back with you.' Vinnie stood up and rolled up the blanket, then stuffed it into his rucksack. 'I am beat.'

'Are you sure? I'll be all right on my own.' Christopher pushed himself up out of the chair and wrapped Bobby's lead around his hand.

'I'm sure.' Vinnie nodded. 'I won't sleep if I don't know you got home safe.'

Christopher chuckled. 'All right then. But I may insist you come in for a nightcap.'

'Oh go on then, twist my arm.' Vinnie laughed.

They said their farewells, then Vinnie and Christopher walked up the beach together with Bobby trotting between them. They were clearly chatting away as they walked, and it made Rosa smile.

'Are you tired?' she asked Henry.

'A little. But I think I have another hour left in me.'

He leant on his knees and the glow of the flames highlighted his handsome face, played across his skin like a golden caress. Rosa gazed at him, not minding if he noticed now, emboldened by the darkness and the cider, by the time spent together and by Christopher's confession. Time really did wait for no one, and it was important to grab happiness when you could.

'So ... The Book Nook,' he said. 'Tell me about it.'

'What do you mean?' she asked.

'Well ... It's a little slice of heaven. With the ambient lighting, reading chairs, coffee machine and all the beautiful books, it's a haven for book lovers. It's cosy and comforting, some could say it's even womb-like. What inspired you to create a retreat like that?'

Rosa sat back and stared at the fire. She hadn't even thought about the shop like that and now Henry had spelt it out for her; she realised that was exactly what she had done. Owning her own bookshop was a lifelong dream, naturally, but she hadn't pictured it feeling womb-like. And yet, it was. She could see that now. She had created a safe space for people, providing everything a booklover could need and want. It wasn't just a shop; it was a retreat, and Henry had seen that straight away. The Book Nook was warm, quiet and cocooning; a soothing place where people could relax, learn and grow.

'I guess I just wanted a safe space for me and for others. Growing up, I had my aunt who I adored, but I missed my parents. I missed what I could have had with them.'

'What happened?'

'My father was just … not on the scene. He emigrated when I was young and my mother was killed in an accident at work.'

'I'm sorry.'

She met his eyes. 'She knew the risks.'

'What did she do?' He placed his hands on his knees and gazed at her intently.

'She was a stunt performer.'

'Wow!'

'I know, right?' Rosa smiled. 'Not a regular mum job.'

'So she passed away doing a stunt?'

Rosa nodded. 'She was only twenty-three, and I was six. She was young having me. My aunt was looking after me while Mum was away working and I still remember the day of the phone call. Mum was in Texas on a movie set when she jumped from a moving vehicle as part of a stunt for a car chase scene. She uhhh … it went wrong, and she was badly injured and died soon after. The injuries she sustained were fatal, and that was that.' She sighed and hugged herself as she said the words. Even though it had been a long time ago, she still found it hard to tell people about it. Her mother had been beautiful, brave, wild, and somewhat reckless. 'Mum was exciting and energetic and the opposite of my sensible aunt. She lived fast and loved danger, and her job was every-thing to her. I was … an afterthought, an inconvenience that could have stopped her doing the job she loved, but luckily for her, my aunt stepped up and cared for me.'

'I'm sorry that you had to go through that and that you lost your mum.'

'Thanks. I was lucky, though. Aunt Jocelyn was wonderful, and I had a great life with her. There were times when I'd wish my mum was there, but as an adult I can see that I really wouldn't have been better off living with my mum. She simply wasn't mother material.' She shrugged. 'Jocelyn, however, was. And as for my dad … What are you going to do? You can't make someone love you and some people shouldn't have children. End of…'

'That's true.' Henry nodded. 'It's not for everyone.'

'What about you? I know you have a mum as I was there at the café when she phoned, but what about other family?'

Henry sat up straight and pushed a hand through his hair. 'I have both parents alive. I grew up with them and my younger sister in Reading. My childhood was pretty uneventful, really. Dad always had a clear vision of what he wanted for me and he drummed into me that a strong work ethic, self-discipline and ambition were key to success. As a teen, I rebelled a bit, but nothing major. I kind of always knew I'd do what I could to make the old man happy. And so I went into finance in London and worked as an investment banker.'

'And how did that go?'

'I hated it.' He gave a wry laugh. 'Hated every single day of it and knew I needed to get out and do something I enjoyed. The money was great, yes, but the boredom and the sense of anxiety I had all the time just made it unbearable. And…' He bit his lower lip.

'And?'

'It was my father's plan and not mine, just like with my romantic life.'

'Oh.' Rosa gave a slow nod then turned back to the firepit, not wanting him to feel under pressure to tell her more.

'My mum is lovely. She's nurturing and empathetic, but she's run herself ragged over the years trying to maintain peace. She puts everyone's needs before her own and even worked as a counsellor for young carers, which meant she was helping people at work and at home. I don't think her own childhood was great and so she wanted it to be different for me and my sister, Megan, but with my dad it was hard to get the balance right.'

'What made you decide you had to change your job?' Rosa asked, feeling that should be a safe enough question, seeing as how he hadn't elaborated on the topic of romance.

'That is … complicated.'

'Sorry. Don't feel you have to tell me.'

Henry shuffled closer to her and took her hand between both of his. 'I don't feel I have to, but I would like to tell you.'

His skin was warm and his hands felt huge compared to hers. Next to him, she felt petite and feminine, protected and alive. It was like all her nerves were firing because he was close. She could smell him, a heady combination of mint, geranium, and something else … ambergris. The scent was fresh and rich and warm, and she wondered if it would smell even better if she were wrapped in his arms with her face against his warm neck.

'I was in a relationship from my early twenties with a childhood friend. Shona was also the daughter of my father's golfing buddy. She was raised to be highly competitive, and this seeped into all areas of her life. When we were in our twenties, it was exciting and fun and I thought it would be fine, but as I got older and started to feel like I couldn't stay in finance, the cracks in our relationship grew. Shona wanted everything to be perfect. She had our lives mapped out, from our career paths to our wedding to how many children we would have and even what their names would be. Now, for her, that was comforting because it fed her need for control, but for me … It was terrifying. I felt trapped and hemmed in and like I couldn't breathe some days. I'm quite easy-going and went along with it for a while, but then … when I thought about changing career and becoming a teacher, she was very negative. She said teachers earned little, and she wanted money and a big house and holidays and private schools for our children. It dawned on me that I was living her dream life and not my own, and when it hit me that this was the case, I knew I had to change something.'

'But it's hard leaving a relationship, right? Whatever's going on, walking away from what you know is difficult.'

'Incredibly difficult and I didn't want to hurt her. I cared about her and the thought of ruining her dream wasn't one I relished.'

'So what did you do?' Rosa watched his face, the way a tiny muscle in his jaw twitched and his eyes closed for a moment as he remembered.

'I kept trying at work, but then one day, I could barely get out of bed. I knew I had to change something. She wasn't happy when I told her I was going to train as a teacher, whether she liked it or not, but she stayed with me and we kept going. I got a job and started teaching in London. Shona's plans had fallen by the wayside by that point and there was a distance growing between us. I knew there was, but I didn't know what to do about it because I felt responsible for creating it. Then, a few years into my new career, I was on a coach taking some pupils on a trip when I saw her with another man. A mutual friend from school. They were coming out of a hotel in the afternoon, holding hands and laughing, and as the coach passed them, they kissed. Of course, I was unable to get off the coach, so I sat there and tried to make sense of what I'd seen. She'd been staying out a lot, claiming to be with friends or her parents, and she'd apparently holidayed with friends too, but I think I was too afraid to delve deeper because of what I could find out.'

'I'm sorry, Henry. That must have hurt.'

'It did but not as much as it would have done had I carried on living a lie. I'd made some changes and so had she, but while mine were career orientated, hers involved finding a new man.' He laughed, then sighed. 'What can you do, right? I loved her, but was I in love with her by the end? Honestly, I don't know. I cared about her and didn't want to hurt her and I think that she didn't want to hurt me. She just didn't know how to end things when it came down to it. And that was three years ago. It takes a while to accept that things are over emotionally, and then when you own a home together, there's all the things to sort out financially and practically. It meant that things dragged on for a bit before we could finally say goodbye. I carried on in my job in London until one morning I woke up and realised I didn't have to stay there. As a single man in possession of a good fortune… I must be in want of a new life.' He winked at her. 'See what I did there?'

'I do!' She laughed.

'So I realised I could live anywhere and started looking for jobs and … here I am.' He squeezed her hand.

'And where is Shona now?'

'Married with a baby on the way. We still speak on the phone now and then, but it's like we've only ever been friends. I don't think she was ever my person, nor I hers, but we got together young because our fathers were friends. Shona needed a level of control over life that I couldn't cope with. She even hated me reading so much because she said it took me away from her and from planning things.'

'That's not good.'

'I know. I mean … reading is something I enjoy, it relaxes me and gives my mind a break from everything else, but she didn't want me escaping into books or cluttering her home with them.'

Rosa shuddered. 'I couldn't live with someone who said that to me.'

'It wasn't great. But now I can read all I want and buy as many books as I like and it's wonderful. Any future partner will have to love books as much as I do.'

He held Rosa's gaze as he released her hand so he could stroke her cheek, then cup her chin. He moved closer, his eyes on her mouth, then he kissed her; she barely felt their lips touch because the kiss was so gentle.

'Books are life,' she said, her eyes fixed on his mouth.

'Books are everything,' he replied, then he kissed her again, this time sliding his hand around the back of her neck and tangling his fingers in her hair.

When he released her, they gazed at each other as if seeing for the first time. Rosa felt breathless with desire and affection and also with surprise. She liked Henry but hadn't really believed things between them could progress like this, but it seemed he liked her too. And yet he had things in his past that could make him hold back — as did she.

'What about you?' he asked. 'Do you have any history of relationships that made you wonder if you ever wanted to settle down?'

Rosa licked her lips and scanned his face. He'd just told her some important things about himself and now he wanted to learn about her too, but the thought of telling him about what had happened, about bringing that into this moment, seemed wrong.

'I … uhm…' She pressed her lips together and held her breath.

'Hey, it's OK. There's no pressure for you to tell me. It can wait until you're ready or you can just pack it away in your past if you like. I just want you to know that you can talk to me whenever you like. It won't scare me or make me see you differently. I really like you and care for you and would like to see where this goes between us.'

She nodded as she exhaled, then turned back to the firepit. When Henry slid his arm around her shoulders, she snuggled closer to him, savouring his warmth and the fact that right now, he liked her. If she told him what had happened before, then it could change how he saw her and she didn't want that to happen. She liked the way Henry viewed her, without prejudice or distaste, but if she told him about her ex and what had happened, he might think there was something wrong with her and that she wasn't worth making an effort for. And that would be devastating. So for now, she'd enjoy this time with Henry, and one day, if she felt it was the right time, then she would share.

And only then…

17

HENRY

*H*enry had been for a run and was making his
way home when he paused on the coastal path
to look out at the sea. The past three weeks had flown by and
he'd been loving village life. He'd been seeing more of Rosa
and enjoying her company, but they were still taking things
slow. He'd shared with her why he'd come to Cornwall and
what had happened with Shona, but Rosa hadn't told him
much about her past, other than about her mum's tragic
death and her father's neglect of the fact that he even had a
daughter. That would be enough to leave a person scarred,
but he suspected there was more. When he'd asked about her
romantic relationships, she'd clammed up, so he'd told her
not to worry and that they could talk about it if she ever felt
ready to share.

He wanted to know more about her and to understand her,
but he also knew that these things could take time and he
was in no rush.

As he gazed out over the sea, it hit him how quiet everything
was. He'd seen on the weather forecast that there was a

storm coming in, but ran anyway because he wanted to get his heart rate up and to burn off some of the excess energy he had.

The copper-grey sky pressed down, the air heavy and humid despite it being late October. It reminded him of the humidity of summer when thunder and lightning seemed to come out of nowhere, but this was worse because there was a sense of unease in the air. Call it a primal under-standing of what was to come or not — something was telling him he needed to rush home before the heavens opened.

When he got back to the village, the wind had picked up and it swirled around his ankles, moaned through the cobbled streets, and made the hairs on his arms stand up under his running top. There was something coming and he had a feeling it was going to be rough. The boats in the harbour were rocking wildly now rather than bobbing like they usually did, and the creaking timbers of their hulls were starting to protest. Waves slapped against their sides sending up salty spray and the air seemed heavy with the scent of fish, tar and the tide.

Before heading for home, he went via the bookshop and peered through the window. Rosa was behind the counter, so he knocked the glass.

'You OK?' he asked when she opened the door.

She nodded, but there was something in her eyes that made his gut churn. 'It will be OK.'

'I hope so. I hate storms. The forecast said we're getting the end of a tropical storm and it could be quite severe. I've moved the window displays and turned off the computer, but I'm still anxious about it.'

'Of course you are. But everything will be OK. I guess we need to get used to storms now that we're living here.' He smiled in an attempt at reassuring her, but Rosa chewed at a nail uncertainly.

'Look … I just need to pop home and shower, then I'll come back and spend the evening with you if you like.'

Rosa blinked and inhaled slowly. 'There's no need. You said in your message earlier that you were going to check on Christopher. That's more important than holding my hand.' She smiled but it didn't reach her eyes. 'Please check that he's OK, and that Bobby is safe. He likes to sniff around the garden and I'd hate to think of him outside in this.'

'No problem. I'll head straight to Christopher's after my shower. Just phone if you need me.'

'I will.'

He turned to go.

'Henry!' Rosa rushed over to him. 'Please be careful.'

'Of course.' He pressed a hand to her cheek and kissed her forehead. He was conscious of being sweaty and didn't want to embrace her because of that, but he was worried about her and wished he could stay and comfort her. However, he knew she would worry about Christopher too so he'd make sure the elderly man and his dog were safe and later on, he'd come back to Rosa.

18

ROSA

*R*osa had done everything she could downstairs in the shop other than board up the windows and she'd considered that, but it also seemed kind of dramatic. Standing in the front window of the flat that overlooked the street and the harbour, she watched as the sky turned dark as a fresh bruise and the boats in the harbour strained at their moorings like horses at a rodeo. The window glass seemed to shiver in its frame, and she hoped it had been fitted securely because she certainly didn't want her front window falling onto the street below.

She put her cooling mug of tea down on the coffee table and then walked through the flat, checking all the other windows were shut tight. In the bathroom, the water in the toilet rippled, and the building seemed to groan as the wind buffeted it from outside.

And then the flat went dark as the power shut off. The hum of the fridge in the kitchen ceased, leaving behind a heavy silence that was broken only by the howling of the wind outside.

Rosa pressed herself against an internal wall, holding her breath as she listened.

When the rain began, pelting the roof and the windows like tiny pebbles thrown from all angles, she swallowed a moan. She looked up as if afraid the ceiling would fall in and covered her mouth with a hand as fear gripped her.

Thinking of Christopher and Henry, she returned to the lounge and looked for her phone. She located it on the shelf next to the book she'd been reading yesterday, grabbed it, and examined the screen. There was no signal. She was here, alone, cut off from the people she cared about.

A sudden crash from downstairs made her scream, and she placed her hands on her chest as she listened. What had happened? What should she do?

She couldn't stay upstairs unaware of what was happening in her shop, so she opened the door, descended the stairs, and pushed open the internal door that led to The Book Nook.

It was dark, but she felt the chill of the wind on her face and arms and then the cold intensified as she reached the front of the shop. Something had broken the glass of the door and the wind and rain were hurtling in along with the debris that was being thrown around outside like paper confetti.

She looked around for something to cover the hole with, but apart from flimsy posters, there was nothing big enough. Instead, she ran to the reading chairs and grabbed the blankets from them that she'd placed there to make customers comfortable while they read, and carried them to the front of the shop. She covered the shelves that were exposed to the elements and held the blankets there as if she could hold off the storm herself.

It felt like she stood there for hours, holding blankets in place and feeling the icy sting of the rain needling at her skin and the anger of the wind as it clawed at the doorframe. But she wouldn't give up on her shop, her books, her dream. Everything she'd had in life had been taken away from her, piece by piece, but this was hers and she wasn't letting go. She anchored herself there, refusing to surrender.

19

HENRY

*H*enry had showered and dressed quickly, then pulled on his raincoat and boots and hurried to Christopher's just as the storm was really getting going. He'd knocked on the front door, but there had been no answer, so he'd gone around the back and found the door open. After calling for Christopher, he'd gone inside and called again and heard a noise deep within the bowels of the house.

He'd found Christopher in the cellar holding a candle as he searched for camping lights. He helped him look and after they'd located some, they'd gone back upstairs using one of the camping lights to guide their way.

'Where's Bobby?' he'd asked, realising that he hadn't seen the dog since he arrived.

'He went out to the garden and then the power went off. I knew we'd need a light and as you can see, there are candles here, but then I remembered I had camping lights in the cellar. Hasn't Bobby come back inside?' Christopher's brow furrowed, the harsh white glow of the LED lamp etching deep shadows into the lines of his face, turning his wrinkles into narrow ravines.

'I'll do a quick check around downstairs.' Henry placed the camping lights on the kitchen table and turned the rest of them on. 'Why don't you take one of these and go and sit by the fire in the lounge and stay warm?'

'He could be upstairs so it's worth checking up there too,' Christopher said.

Henry was concerned because the elderly man looked gaunt, his face seeming thinner than usual as the bright light accentuated his cheekbones and sharp jawline.

'Let's get you warm first.' He led Christopher to the lounge and settled him into a chair by the fire, then wrapped a blanket around his bony shoulders and draped another over his knees. At least the fire would keep him warm, and he wasn't reliant on an electric one.

He went from room to room, searching for Bobby but he wasn't anywhere inside, not even the cellar which he checked twice just in case he'd gone inside a box or underneath a shelf. Despair filled him because it was clear that the dog must have gone outside and possibly run off.

Back in the lounge, he said, 'Christopher, I'm going out to look for Bobby. He's not in the house, so he could be in the garden somewhere, perhaps sheltering under a bush.'

'I'll come with you,' Christopher pushed himself up, but Henry shook his head.

'Stay there in case he comes back inside. I'll be quicker alone.'

He went to the back door that was propped open in case Bobby had come back while he was upstairs and grabbed a towel from the radiator to mop the floor. The rain lashed in and he knew he'd need to close the door or the kitchen would be flooded. If Bobby came back while he was outside, he'd have to wait.

He pulled the door closed behind him and looked around at the garden that was lit only by brief flashes of moonlight that appeared between the racing clouds. The trees bowed low, their branches creaking and groaning. Leaves, twigs, and other debris swirled in a dizzying, chaotic dance, and a gritty, earthy smell rose in the gusty air. He pulled his hood up and tightened the strings to stop it blowing down, then he began his search of the garden.

Every time he called for the dog, the storm swallowed his voice, and he knew it was futile trying to be heard. He stayed as low as he could, not wanting to be knocked over like the deck chair he saw flying through the street on his way there, and scanned under bushes and trees, trying to work out where the small dog could be hiding.

He was about to go back to the house and start again when something caught his eye at the far end of the garden near the shed, so he fought the wind to get over there.

20

ROSA

*R*osa had struggled for as long as she could to keep the water from the books and then she'd decided that she needed to move them, so she'd lowered the blankets and started taking them to the back of the shop. There, she placed them on the chairs, the tables and on any other free surface so that if the water swept in over the floor, the books would be out of the way.

It took ages because she was trembling from the cold and from anxiety. She inhaled shaky breaths, encountering the smells of salt water, wet paper, ink, and earth. The metallic taste of fear filled her mouth and sat on her tongue like a corrosive penny.

When she'd finished moving the books, she returned to the front of the shop and stared out at the street. The sea had become furious and lashed the village with its power, throwing sea foam on the wind and blasting shells, sand, windows, buildings, and anyone foolish enough to be outside.

Rosa grabbed the driest blanket and a handful of pins from the board behind the counter, then she started pinning the blanket over the hole in the window. It moved in and out like a flapping sail, making a sucking noise on each outward movement, but it held fast and would keep the worst of the weather out.

Then she retreated into the shop to sit and wait it out. Damage had been done, but she wouldn't know how much until tomorrow. Sinking onto the floor in front of a bookcase in the children's section, she buried her face in her hands. She would stay there like a captain with his sinking ship, hoping that the storm would pass, hoping that tomorrow would be a brighter day.

21

HENRY

*H*enry had noticed there was a gap in the hedge at the back of Christopher's garden by the shed. It backed onto woodland and so he'd followed a narrow path through the trees at the back of the garden and found a small clearing. There, at the centre, was a hole. It was about the size of an access hole over a drain and looked like the surface had just given way.

If it was some sort of sinkhole and Bobby had fallen into it, Henry had no idea what the dog's chances would be. He felt sick to his stomach and the back of his throat burned with bile. Shining the torch on his phone over the hole, he peered into it, but it was hard to see clearly with the rain lashing down and the wind blowing things around.

He looked at his phone screen, wanting to check if Rosa was OK, but he had no signal so he'd have to wait until he could get back there. Either that or he could check on her now and then come back and—

Wait. What was that?

He held his breath and listened and when the wind died down a little, he could hear it again.

Whimpering.

He cupped his hands around his mouth and leant over the hole, then shouted, 'Bobby! Hey boy!'

A bark came in reply.

'Bobby! Don't worry, I'm coming for you!'

He had no choice. He couldn't leave the small dog, Christopher's entire world, trapped underground. The poor dog would be terrified, and anything could happen to him if Henry didn't get him out.

'I'm coming boy!' He shouted into the hole.

He crouched down on the ground and lowered his legs into the hole, then he slid into it, still holding his phone and asking the universe to help him out here. If he got stuck too, then at least Bobby would have some company.

He slid through the small opening and landed on his feet in a space the width of a phone box. Because the space was barely five feet high, he had to bend over, but he shone his torch around and saw that it was part of a tunnel. The smell of wet wood, rotting seaweed and old tides enveloped him and he wretched at its strength.

'Bobby?' he called out, and a bark rewarded him. 'Where are you?'

The bark came again, so he followed the noise along the tunnel until he came to what he realised was a cave. And there, trembling in a corner, was the little dog.

'Come here, boy,' he whispered, crouching down.

Bobby whimpered, so he went closer and held out a hand. Bobby sniffed it then wagged his little tail, but he was clearly scared by what had happened and freezing cold. Henry lifted him tenderly, unzipped his jacket and tucked Bobby inside it, then zipped it up again. At least this way Bobby would have the benefit of Henry's body heat and hopefully feel more secure.

Henry shone the phone torch around with one hand while supporting Bobby with the other and he realised he was in an old smugglers' cave. He had heard rumours of smugglers' tunnels beneath many coastal areas of Cornwall, but he'd never been in one before, and he was fascinated.

However, he reminded himself; it was time to get back to Christopher and then to Rosa. He could always return to the cave another time and have a good look around.

As he made his way back, he stumbled once when he stepped on something. He was about to kick it out of the way when he realised it was a small bag, so he picked it up and shone the light on it. It looked like it could contain something of interest, so he tucked it into his pocket and carried on, making his way back to the opening in the ground behind Christopher's home. The tunnel was narrow, and the phone light was fading, so he suspected the battery was running low, but it held until he reached the opening. He climbed out, taking care not to squash Bobby on the way.

When he was above ground again, he sucked in the fresh air, grateful to feel the rain on his skin and the wind buffeting him from side to side. He could still smell the dank earth of the tunnel and cave, still feel the chill in his bones from being down there, but Bobby was safe and he needed to get him warm and dry.

He hurried along the garden and through the back door, put the phone on the table and kicked off his muddy boots, then unzipped his coat and grabbed a towel from the radiator and folded it around Bobby.

'Christopher!' he called. 'I'm back.'

In the lounge, Christopher was waiting in his chair and when he saw Bobby, he clapped his hands and his eyes glistened in the firelight. 'Oh my boy,' he said as opened his arms.

Henry set Bobby on Christopher's lap and he wrapped the blanket he had around him around Bobby too.

'He could do with a wash, but he needed to see you first,' Henry said.

'How is he so muddy?' Christopher asked, not seeming bothered by the fact as he hugged the small dog to him.

'He'd fallen down a hole at the rear of your garden. It was past the trees and in a small clearing.' Henry stood in front of the fire and warmed his hands, his legs, and then turned and did his back.

'That damned hole.' Christopher shook his head. 'I covered it over years ago, but the planks must have moved. I think there's a tunnel under there that probably leads to a smugglers' cave. Smugglers' caves exist in the area, but no one has used them for a very long time. The hole is out of the way so I didn't think it would be a danger to anyone and Bobby rarely goes far from my side. He must have been spooked by the storm and fallen into it.'

'It seemed that way. He'd gone along the tunnel to the cave and was completely bewildered.'

'Thank goodness you found him. I'd be broken without him and the thought of him being down there, terrified and lone, is dreadful.'

'He'll need some TLC over the next few days, and we could get him checked by the vet tomorrow if you're concerned about him, but he's home safe now and that's the main thing.'

'Thank you so much.' Christopher's voice trembled.

'No need for thanks. This is what friends do.' He rubbed at his hair. 'Will you be all right if I check on Rosa? I can come straight back, but I want to make sure she's OK. I don't have any phone signal.'

'The landline is down too,' Christopher said. 'And yes, you must go to her. Bobby and I will be fine now. I'm not letting go of him.'

'I'll get you a drink and some water for him before I leave.' Henry went out to the kitchen and almost cheered at the fact that Christopher had an Aga and that it was sending heat out into the kitchen. First, he put the kettle on the boiling plate; then he filled a bowl with water for Bobby. He quickly made a sandwich in case Christopher hadn't eaten, made tea then placed everything on a tray. He took it through to the lounge and set the bowl on the floor and the mug and sandwich on the table next to Christopher.

'I promise I'll be back as soon as I can,' he said. 'Make sure you drink your tea while it's warm and eat the sandwich.'

'I will, Henry. Your father must be a very proud man,' Christopher said. 'You're a credit to him and your mother.'

Henry coughed as his automatic reply lodge in his throat. He'd love it if his father was proud of him, but he knew that wasn't the case and never would be. 'I'll see you soon,' he said softly, gently patting Christopher's shoulder and then giving Bobby's head a stroke.

He retrieved his coat from the kitchen and pulled it on, then tugged the hood over his head and opened the back door again.

It was going to be a long night, but he was determined to make sure that the people he cared about in Porthpenny were looked after. He'd never forgive himself if anything happened to them when he could have kept them safe. As he marched along the pavement on his way to the bookshop, he realised how much they had come to mean to him — his family of friends that he had found when he least expected it.

He felt fortunate to have met them and hoped they felt the same.

22

ROSA

The morning had finally come and with it the calm after the storm. Rosa stirred in her cocoon on the sofa as she thought about what had happened. Henry had come to her during the night and insisted she go up to the flat and get warm. She'd been shaking from the cold and her clothes had been wet, but she'd barely noticed, so he'd made her take a warm shower and dress in dry clothes. After that, he'd wrapped her up in blankets on the sofa in the flat and warmed her some milk on the gas hob. The power had still been out, so he'd lit the gas with a match. He'd sat with her while she drank the milk and then he'd told her about Bobby and how he'd found him in an old smugglers' cave. After reassuring her that Christopher and Bobby were fine, he stayed with her until she felt sleepy then he'd returned to check on Christopher. He'd also said he would do a tour of the village to see if anyone else needed help. He was such a decent man, and Rosa found his presence comforting, his efforts to help Christopher and Bobby too. If he hadn't been there, Bobby might never have been found, and that would have been absolutely awful.

She roused herself and padded down to the shop to face the damage. The shop was a mess, but Henry was already there tidying things up.

'Hey there.' He stopped what he was doing and came to her side, placed a hand on her arm. 'How're you feeling?'

'More to the point, how are you feeling? Did you get any rest at all?'

He gave a shy smile. 'Not really. Well, half an hour at Christopher's and then I sat in here for a break about an hour ago, but my adrenaline was pumping hard so I've kept going.'

She looked at his pale face, the stubble on his cheeks and the dark shadows under his eyes. 'That adrenaline wearing off now?'

'Kind of…' He winced. 'I guess I'll sleep later.'

'Why don't we go up to the café and see if Pearl has power up there? She has solar panels in part of the gardens, so she may have some electricity even if the mains isn't on yet. We can pick something up for Christopher and drop it off on the way back.'

'That's a great idea. We can't do much here until we refuel, anyway.'

'Exactly. I'll grab a jacket and some boots, and we can get going.'

When she came back down, she saw Henry had filled a black bag, and he'd got the mop from the cupboard and started the clean-up.

'There are some books in the black bag,' he said apologetically. 'We can have a look at them later and see if we can dry them out.'

She bit the inside of her cheek as emotion swelled like a stormy sea inside her. 'I tried to protect them.'

'I know you did, and you saved most of them, but a few got wet and dirty. It must have happened when the glass in the door first smashed.'

'I should have been better prepared.'

'I think the ferocity of the storm took most people by surprise. And the forecasters were saying it could go either way. Hedging their bets, I guess.'

'I need to get the glass in the door fixed.' She sagged as a sense of hopelessness washed over her. This was her fresh start, and it had already been tarnished.

'We can do that. I've boarded it up for now, though.' He gestured at the front of the shop and she saw he had fitted a board over the window and secured it in place.

'Thank you so much. When did you do that?'

'Earlier. When the rain stopped.'

'You're amazing, Henry.'

'I don't know about that, but I do what I can.' He stifled a yawn and rubbed at his eyes. 'I need coffee.'

'Me too. Come on, then.'

They went out into the street, and Rosa looked around. The morning was pale and damp, the air cold and clammy. The sky was dove grey with layers of clouds and the water in the harbour looked brown and frothy. Debris littered the streets, a combination of leaves, twigs, mud and other things, including a car wing mirror, a sock, and an assortment of feathers. She hoped no birds had been injured and that they had found sufficient shelter during the storm.

Rosa stopped walking and turned to Henry. She took hold of his shoulders and gazed into his eyes. 'This could have been so much worse. The outcome, I mean.'

He nodded. His Adam's apple bobbed.

She pulled him closer and moved her hands so they rested on his cheeks, needing to touch him and to feel his warmth. 'You were out in that storm most of the night. You could have been hurt.' Her eyes stung at the thought and she rubbed her thumbs over his jaw, his cheeks and slid them into his hair, then she moved to her tiptoes and leant closer to him. When she kissed him, she sighed against him and felt their bodies mould together as if made to fit. As if he was the missing piece of her jigsaw.

Last night, instead of hiding away and making sure that he was OK, Henry had come to her, gone to Christopher and Bobby. He had checked in with both of them and not even thought about his own safety. He had put them first, and she was overwhelmed with gratitude and more. She kissed him hard, enveloped him in her arms, not wanting to ever let him go. No man had ever done something like this for her before and now, here was Henry, everything she had ever imagined in a future life partner, and he was looking out for her. Selflessly. Without judgement. With kindness and affection. Plus, he was hot as hell and she found him irresistible.

When she finally leant back to look at him again, he was smiling, and there was something in his eyes that made her core flutter.

'What was that for?' he asked, not taking his eyes off her.

'I'm just so happy you're OK. If you'd been hurt, I...' A tear trickled down her left cheek, and he gently wiped it away with his thumb.

'I'm fine. I was careful.' He kissed her. 'Very careful. And we got through it, sweetheart. Together. Everything will be OK.'

She sighed as she rested her head on his chest, feeling for the first time in a long time that she could trust someone, could lean on him, could believe that he was who he said he was. Henry had told her that everything would be OK and she would choose to believe that because it felt a lot better than worrying that he was trying to deceive her. It felt a lot better than managing alone.

*T*hey walked up to The Garden Café, looking at the damage caused by the storm on the way. The damage consisted primarily of debris and water; fortunately, most buildings and boats remained undamaged. The book-shop was a small, detached building, so it had caught the worst of the wind blowing into the cove and Henry said he suspected the door window must have been loose in its frame to have smashed like that.

At the café, there was some mess in the gardens, but the high hedges and trees that surrounded the gardens had provided a protective barrier, and so the café itself was fine. Inside, they found other villagers who'd come for breakfast after waking to find their power was off.

'Good morning, lovelies.' Pearl came from behind the counter and opened her arms. 'Rosa, I'm so sorry to hear about the damage to the bookshop. If there's anything we can to do help, just say.' She hugged Rosa tight and Rosa's eyes stung.

'Thank you,' she murmured against Pearl's shoulder. 'That's very kind. We haven't finished cleaning up yet so I'm not sure how much damage was done but the window in the door needs replacing.'

'Well, I know a man who can do that for you!' Pearl said. 'Give me a moment.'

Pearl crossed the café and spoke to a group of men wearing overalls, and one of them nodded. When she came back to them, she said, 'It's all sorted. Peter will be there later to replace the window and to check the others.'

Rosa swallowed down the question about the cost because it was something she'd have to cover for now, but hoped the insurance would repay it once the claim had processed.

'And don't worry, he said it won't cost a penny.' Pearl smiled.

'How come?' Rosa asked.

'He does odd jobs around the village and said he has a pane of glass that will fit your door perfectly. Or, if you'd prefer, a replacement door.'

'It might be an idea to get the door replaced,' Henry said. 'That one is quite old, and the wood looks like it's seen better days.'

'Worth thinking about,' Pearl said. 'But for now, let me get you some breakfast and coffee and you can take a breather. You both look beat.' She patted Henry's arm, then returned to the counter.

Within ten minutes, Henry, and Rosa were sitting at a table with mugs of coffee and bacon rolls in front of them. Rosa ate like she was famished and felt the coffee reviving her sip by sip. She'd swallowed her last bite when she sat upright, as if shocked by a lightning bolt. 'Christopher! We need to take him something. I bet he hasn't even had a cup of tea this morning.'

'He'll be fine,' Henry said. 'He has the Aga, and that was heating water and the kitchen last night. And he had the fire lit in the lounge and lots of blankets wrapped around him and Bobby.'

'Oh … of course. I'd forgotten about those older sources of heat. Thank goodness he has them.'

'There's a lot to be said for not relying on mains energy.' Henry nodded. 'When the power goes out, we're stranded.'

'I think we should see him, though.' Rosa stood up. 'I'll just get him some breakfast.'

After she'd bought a bacon roll for Christopher and a sausage for Bobby, she thanked Pearl and gave her number to Peter Harkness, who seemed like a pleasant man. In his fifties, with grey hair and silver framed glasses, he was a portly man with a cheerful demeanour. She'd seen him around the village wearing his navy overalls and knew he worked with his daughter, Hattie, who was currently speaking to Ellie outside the café.

Rosa and Henry made their way down to Christopher's home and knocked on the door. He answered with Bobby in his arms and smiled.

'There you both are. What a delight it is to see you after such a terrible night.'

They went inside to the kitchen where Christopher had made a pot of tea and sat at the kitchen table. The large rectangular oak table had some worn and faded patches and when Rosa placed a hand on the wood, she could feel indents that had been made over the years. There were scars on it from cutlery, where she suspected someone had slipped with a knife while cutting vegetables. She traced the grooves with a finger, recognising words forming a list or letter. In several places, someone had placed something hot on the surface without a protective mat. But she liked that the table had a history, that people had used and loved it, and that it had been the centre of a family kitchen for many years. It had character, just like Christopher, and she hoped that one day she would have a similar table in her kitchen that her own family could sit at while they ate, talked and worked. She'd always dreamt of having children who would do their homework while she made dinner, sharing details of their day as she listened attentively, proud of them for being such amazing human beings. It was traditional, yes, this yearning she'd had to have a family, but she was OK with that. And yet when she'd first hoped to create this dream with her ex, she'd had no idea what was going on that would prevent her dream coming true. The thought made her head hurt, and so she pushed the memories away like storm debris. This was not the time or place for feeling sad at what had gone before.

Christopher set Bobby down in his basket, then brought the pot of tea and some mugs to the table and Rosa got his bacon roll and the sausage for Bobby out of the paper bag. She set them on the table and Christopher chuckled.

'Well, thank you very much. This looks and smells delightful. I'm guessing it's all organic if it's come from Pearl and Ellie.'

'Of course.' Rosa smiled. 'Organic, free range and as fresh as could be.'

Christopher sat down and called Bobby over. 'Your Aunty Rosa has a treat for you.'

While Rosa fed the sausage to Bobby, Christopher ate his bacon roll and Henry filled him in about the storm damage. Most people had only been affected by the power cut, but at the café, he'd been speaking to the former footballer, Thomas Dryden, and his partner, Lena Teller, and they'd told him that the villagers were planning a community cleanup that afternoon. They all needed to help, so they would meet in the square at noon.

Christopher nodded. 'It's always been the way. We've had some terrible storms over the years, like the one of 1962 when Cornwall took a battering from the elements. Worst affected was Penzance, but a lot of the coast was hit by high winds and heavy rain that caused damage and flooding. And then there were the storms of 2013 and 2014 that caused over 20 million pounds worth of damage to Cornwall. It's an amazing part of the world to live but it suffers when storms come because of how exposed it is. However, at times like this, seeing the communities come together and rally around one another is uplifting.'

'Last night was scary,' Rosa said, cradling her mug of tea. 'But Henry was incredible.'

'A real hero,' Christopher agreed. 'Saving Bobby like that with no thought for your own safety…' He shook his head. 'That was an act of bravery indeed.'

Henry blushed and rubbed at the back of his neck. 'I only did what anyone would have done.'

'Don't believe that, lad.' Christopher frowned. 'Not everyone would risk themselves for a dog. To some, they'd see Bobby as *just a dog*, but he's all I've got. He's my family, and you saved him. I don't know how I'll ever thank you.'

'I wasn't really thinking about anything other than finding him and getting him safe.' Henry reached down and stroked Bobby, then lifted him and sat him on his lap. 'He's a precious little man and there was no way I could leave him out there alone in that weather.'

Bobby turned and placed his paws on Henry's chest then gave his cheek a lick. Henry stroked his small head, then wrapped his arms around him and Bobby settled down for a nap.

'Thank you for my breakfast.' Christopher picked up his mug of tea. 'Best bacon roll I've ever had.'

'You're very welcome.' Rosa smiled.

After they'd drunk two pots of tea, Rosa stood and stretched. 'I should get back to the shop and assess the damage for the insurance company. Peter Harkness is coming to fit a new window or even a new door and I need to air the shop and dry what I can.'

'Of course.' Christopher nodded. 'Why don't you two let me cook you dinner this evening as a thank you?'

Rosa looked at Henry, and he nodded. 'That would be awesome. Do you need me to pick anything up?'

Christopher shook his head. 'I have everything I need here. Come over around six and I'll have everything ready.'

Rosa and Henry hugged Christopher, and Bobby, then walked back to the bookshop. When they got there, she was surprised to see that Peter and Hattie were already waiting for her. Meanwhile, along the street, people worked with brushes and hose pipes, cleaning the road and pavements and windows of houses and shops. She unlocked the door and let Peter and Hattie inside while she went to the counter and leant against it, then looked around.

'It's a bit messy, but nothing we can't fix,' Henry said as he stood next to her.

'You already did some of it earlier or it would look a lot worse.' Rosa hugged herself as she gazed at the shop that had seemed so full of promise and dreams just two months ago. How quickly dreams could sour and how quickly life could change.

And then she looked at the man standing at her side, at his solid form and the way he was rolling up his sleeves ready to get stuck in, and she knew that whatever life threw at her, she would be OK. She'd been through a lot already, not as much as some but more than others, but she was still here. She was starting over and this was just a blip, a test of her resilience, and goodness only knew she had plenty of that to keep her going.

Rosa Resilience Lake, her aunt had often called her, and now the thought made her laugh.

'Oh!' Henry said as he patted his jacket pocket. 'I almost forgot about this.'

He pulled a small velvet bag from his pocket and held it out. 'I found this in the cave when I was looking for Bobby and I thought you might like it.'

'What is it?' She eyed the bag.

'Take a look.' He handed the bag to her, and she loosened the drawstring and peered inside.

She pulled out a small carved wooden rose the size of her palm. 'This is beautiful.'

'I thought you could put it up in here. A rose for Rosa.' His cheeks coloured, and he lowered his gaze to the floor. 'Only if you like it, that is.'

'Is it OK for me to keep it, though? If you found it in the cave, I mean.'

'I guess so. It could have been dropped there or washed up from the sea at some point, just like anything we find on the beach. It's not necessarily an antique of any financial value.' He gave a small shrug, and she smiled.

'It is of value to me because you found it and now you've gifted it to me. I will treasure it.' She held it against her heart and reached out her free hand and touched his cheek. 'Are you always this sweet and kind?'

He blinked, and the blush in his cheeks deepened. 'I uhm … I don't know.' He looked down, then back up again and held her gaze. 'Perhaps you bring it out in me.'

'Well, I think you're the sweetest man I've ever met.' She looked over at the doorway where Peter and Hattie were measuring the opening. 'But I also feel scared because … I wonder if this could end up going wrong. I'm so scared of being hurt.'

She clutched the rose tighter, the confession hard to share, but she felt that now was the right time.

'I won't hurt you,' he said. 'You have my word.'

She exhaled the breath she hadn't realised she was holding and stepped closer to him, rested her head on his chest. Trusting others wasn't easy, and she didn't know if she could fully commit to trusting Henry, but she knew she owed it to him to try. He was a good man, and he'd done nothing to suggest otherwise, but then she also knew that sometimes people weren't what they seemed to be.

He stroked her hair, then whispered, 'Come on. Let's get this shop spick and span so we can enjoy dinner with Christopher.'

She nodded, then stepped back and placed the rose on a shelf behind the counter where she could see it every day. Where, when she looked at it, she would be reminded of the first Cornish storm she'd experienced and how she'd overcome it with Henry's help and support. He was proving himself to be a supportive friend to her, and she hoped she was reading the signs correctly that there could, perhaps, be something more growing between them.

How wonderful that would be…

23

HENRY

*I*t had been ten days since the storm, and Henry had seen a lot of Rosa as he'd helped her to get the bookshop back to the way it had been. He'd been at school for some of the time, but now it was half term, so he'd be able to spend more time with Rosa, taking her food and drinks and making himself useful.

Rosa was, he thought, an incredible woman. She'd grown up living with her aunt after losing her mum. Her father was absent, demonstrating a lack of love and affection, and that would be hard for anyone to deal with. Henry knew first-hand how difficult it was to have a father who could be hard and cold, but to have no sign that you mattered to a parent would be even worse. Listening to Rosa speak about her mum had made him believe she admired her bravery, but regretted what it had cost them both. He suspected it had bled into Rosa's romantic life and made her scared of trusting someone with her heart. Her mum had been there one day and gone the next, and that would understandably make a child wary of loving again. If the one person you'd loved as a child was suddenly gone, then how was that supposed to leave you feeling? Alone. Scared. Isolated. Bereft. Her aunt had taken Rosa in and they'd had a good relationship from what she'd told him, but now she'd lost her aunt too. So apart from a distant father, she had no one left. Rosa deserved so much more than that and Henry wanted to see her happy and secure, safe and loved. He was thinking — and wishing — that he could be her person, but he also suspected she would find it hard to trust him with her heart. Add to that the feeling that she was also hiding something else, something that had happened to her that she hadn't yet divulged, and she was a deep river.

And this was why she loved books so much, he was certain of it. He knew how they could provide a refuge from the world, a place where a reader could escape and find comfort. Having that in common with Rosa gave them a special connection, and it was something he believed they could build on together. As he knew, relationships were not easy, but having shared interests and goals gave a couple something special. He hadn't felt that with his ex, but he did feel it with Rosa. With her, he already felt that he could commit to a future, but only if she wanted that too. If not, he would have to be content with friendship. That would be a challenge when he found her so beautiful and wanted to kiss her every time he saw her, but still better than not having her in his life at all. Being around Rosa had made him realise exactly what had been wrong in his relationship with Shona. Committing to her for life had been something he'd been unsure about, but the idea of committing to Rosa made his heart sing.

Before leaving home, he looked in the mirror one last time. He hoped she was going to like what she saw because he'd spent quite a bit of time getting ready this afternoon, and he felt rather silly. But it was Halloween, and they were going to the fancy dress party at the café, so he'd done his best with his costume.

He walked to the bookshop and peered through the window that was decorated with fake cobwebs, pumpkin lights, and small velvet pumpkins. The display featured a range of new books with ghost stories, vampires, and zombies, and horror classics including *Frankenstein, Dracula* and *The Shining*. Rosa was behind the counter with Vinnie and a life-size skeleton wearing glasses and holding a book. He smiled at their costumes. It was like being catapulted into a parallel universe, watching them tidy up and chat away like it was just a normal day like any other. Unable to resist any longer, he opened the door and went inside.

'Ta da!' He held out his hands and watched their faces.

'You look amazing!' Rosa laughed, then came around the counter and looked him up and down. 'What a fabulous costume.'

'You both look amazing, too.'

The three of them, without discussing their costumes, had dressed as zombie pirates and now resembled a motley crew ready to sail the seven seas.

'I think we're ready to set sail, don't you?' Rosa said, and they all laughed.

'How was Christopher?' he asked as they got ready to leave.

'He's all set up.' Rosa pulled her coat on over her costume, careful not to tear the delicate chiffon of the cobwebs around the neckline. 'He has a bucket filled with sweets and Vinnie set pumpkins around the front porch and lining the path. Then we dressed Bobby in his pumpkin costume. I think they'll be fine, but I told him to phone if he has any problems. I think he's looking forward to having some trick or treaters.'

'Brilliant!' Henry liked the thought of Christopher having fun. They'd asked him if he wanted to go to the party at the café, but he'd said he'd be happy at home handing out sweets.

'Ready then?' Henry asked.

'Ready!' Rosa and Vinnie replied.

When they arrived at The Garden Café, they could hear the music from outside on the path. They went through the gate and into the gardens. Small pumpkin lights adorned the hedges and tree branches. Carved pumpkins with gaping mouths, uneven teeth and slanting eyes grinned at them from the path and on tables and benches, as well as from the windows of the café itself. The gardens were busy with people milling around, all of them wearing costumes, and Henry looked at them, trying to work out who they were, but it was difficult, especially with those wearing masks.

'I'm going to see if I can find my family,' Vinnie said.

'Catch you later,' Henry said as Vinnie walked away. 'You OK?' he asked Rosa.

'Yes, thanks. It all looks incredible.' She gazed around them, smiling through her black lipstick.

'Let's get a drink.' He took her hand, and they walked towards the café.

'Mr Clay!' A small boy waved at Henry and he waved back. 'Hello, Paul. Love the costume.'

'Thanks, Sir. My mummy made it out of old boxes.' The boy was wearing a box around his middle and had one on his head with a circle cut out for his face. They had been painted silver with some red patches to suggest he was rusting. Silver paint also covered his face, and antennae protruded from the top of his head box. 'I'm a robot.'

'I can see that.' Henry smiled.

'Is that your wife?' the boy asked.

Henry glanced at Rosa and saw her eyes widen.

'She looks like your wife. You match.' The boy pointed at their costumes.

'I'm his friend,' Rosa stammered as she let go of Henry's hand. 'We're just friends.'

'I think you should get married. You look happy together.' The boy turned around, then glanced at them again. 'Sorry, I better go. My mummy said not to wander off because I can't see very well with the box on my head. She said to stay close so she can stop me bumping into things.'

'You'd better get back to her then,' Henry said. 'Have fun.'

'Thanks, Sir. You too!' The boy shuffled away, and Henry turned to Rosa. 'Sorry about that. He's not in my class, but I know him from school. Children say exactly what's on their minds.'

Rosa chewed at her bottom lip and concern filled him. 'What is it?'

She shook her head.

'Please tell me.'

'I just … I'm not sure, really.'

'Do you like children?' he asked.

'Of course. I couldn't eat a whole one but…' She winked.

'Ha ha! But do you think you'll want children in the future?'

Rosa looked down and brushed at the skirt of her dress as if cleaning something away. She sighed, then met his eyes again. 'It's not always that straightforward, is it? Wanting and having aren't always the same thing.'

Something in her tone told Henry not to push the conversation. He'd only wanted to find out how she felt about having a family because he'd doubted that he would want children, but now, being around Rosa had made him question his prior beliefs.

'Let's get a drink,' he said, reaching for her hand again. When she let him take it, he breathed a sigh of relief because the last thing he wanted was to irritate her or make her anxious when they'd been getting on so well.

Orange cloths covered the tables in the café, with pumpkins in the centre of each one. Small LED lights flickered inside the pumpkins, and fairy lights adorned the counter and windows. The café smelt of cinnamon and ginger and when they went to the counter, he could see why. Green-and-orange iced cupcakes featured bats and ghosts, mini loaves of gingerbread had been decorated to look like coffins and mini cinnamon apple pies had faces carved into their pastry lids.

'Cake?' he asked.

'Please.' Rosa selected one with a bat on it and he got one with a ghost.

'What would you like to drink?' Pearl asked from behind the counter. Dressed as Cruella de Vil, Pearl's outfit was so convincing that Henry had to remind himself she was actually very nice and not a cruel dog thief.

'What have you got?' Rosa asked.

'We have non-alcoholic bloodthirsty punch, which is cranberry juice with lime juice and lemonade. We have Franken-
punch, which is ginger ale, pineapple juice, lime sorbet and
tequila. Finally, we've made caramel apple mimosas, which
contain caramel, cinnamon sugar, apple cider and caramel
vodka.'

'They all sound delicious,' Rosa looked up at Henry. 'What do
you fancy?'

He bit back the reply 'You!' and said, 'I'll have a Franken-
punch, please, Pearl.'

'And I'll have the same,' Rosa said.

Pearl got their drinks, and they took them along with their
cakes to the green leather sofa. Sitting next to each other,
they sipped their drinks simultaneously and Henry felt his
eyes widen. 'Wow!'

'It's so strong.' Rosa licked her lips. 'Delicious but strong.'

'It is indeed,' he said. 'We should drink these, then try the
mimosas too.'

'Really?' She giggled and for a moment, he saw the relaxed
Rosa he adored. She could be so calm and lacking in guile,
but then a wall would shoot up and he'd find it hard to know
what she was thinking. It seemed to happen more often now,
and he wondered if it was because she was confronting feelings she hadn't dealt with for a while. It could happen when
people felt vulnerable. He knew it because he'd felt it himself,
but he wanted Rosa to feel safe with him and not to worry
about being hurt. He had no intention of hurting her. Not
ever.

'Really,' he said. 'We're here to have fun this evening and we
can do whatever we like.'

'I enjoy being with you, Henry,' she said. 'You're fun company and so sweet.'

'Why, thank you.' She covered his hand with hers and leant her head on his shoulder in a way that made his skin grow warm. 'I try to be good company.'

'You are.' She sat up straight again and sipped her drink and Henry did the same, enjoying how the alcohol in the cocktail warmed him right through. Outside in the gardens, people had started dancing and they watched them for a while as they ate their cakes, then Rosa said, 'Want to dance?'

'Why not?'

Rosa led the way outside and they joined in with the dancing. They shimmied around with other zombies, ghosts, vampires, pumpkins, astronauts and more. They danced to *Thriller, Monster Mash, Ghostbusters* and *I Put a Spell on You* … Henry could see Rosa relaxing as she danced, and he was glad. Whatever had happened to her before she came to Cornwall had left its mark, but he hoped she could work through it and have the life she deserved going forwards.

When a slow song came on, Annie Lennox's *Love Song for a Vampire,* Henry held out his hand and Rosa accepted it. She stepped into his embrace and he held her gaze as they moved slowly around on the grass. With the moon high above them, the flickering pumpkins and the air sweet with cinnamon and crisp with autumn, it was a magical moment.

Everything else seemed to fade away, and it was just the two of them and the music.

Their connection.

Their hearts beating as one.

Rosa's eyes glistened and Henry brushed a loose strand of hair from her face before kissing her forehead. Her skin was warm beneath his lips, grounding him in the moment. In awe of the depth of his feelings for this woman, he held her closer. He'd known her just two months, yet he felt as if his soul had always known her and had been waiting for her all this time. Everything that had come before didn't matter because now he was where he was meant to be, and the woman he belonged with was finally in his arms.

When the song finished, they stood still for a few moments as if they both needed to gather their thoughts, and then Rosa said, 'Now, about those caramel apple mimosas.'

'Come on. It would be rude not to try them.' He led her back inside the café and up to the counter, hoping he would be able to do this every Halloween.

24
ROSA

*A*fter drinking the delicious mimosas, Rosa and Henry spent some time socialising with other people at the party. Rosa spoke to Ellie and her partner, Jasper, and to Sita and her husband, Niels. She admired their costumes and those of their children. But try as she might, she couldn't shake off the need to know where Henry was. Her eyes sought him out automatically, her arms longed to hold him again and she missed him, even though he was close by. This depth of feeling surprised her because she'd sworn she'd never allow herself to feel this way again, but it also frightened her. She had never wanted to care for another man again and had thought her resolve would last, but there was something different about Henry and she found she couldn't resist him. It was almost as if they were meant to be together and nothing, not even her fears, could keep them apart. The rational part of her mind screamed at her she was in danger because she was falling deeper for him by the day, but her heart was opening to him and she knew it would be hard now to shut it down.

When Henry returned to her side and took her hand, she almost melted with joy. 'You ready to go?'

'Sure am. Do we need to check in with Christopher?'

She shook her head. 'Vinnie has gone to see him already. He said he'd sort out the pumpkins and help him get settled for the evening.'

'In that case, can I walk you home?'

'I'd like that.'

Their eyes stayed locked for a few moments and then they said their goodbyes and left the gardens. They strolled down the path to the village in silence, their hands still entwined. Rosa thought they must look like ghosts with their pale faces and clothing that resembled rags made of white, black and silver material.

The alcohol she'd consumed thrummed in her veins and she could still taste the cinnamon of the cake and the caramel of the mimosa. The air was chilly and she shivered despite the fact that she'd worn her coat over her costume.

'You're cold,' Henry said, wrapping a big arm around her shoulders and pulling her close. They walked along that way and before she knew it, they were standing on the pavement that overlooked the beach. It was a clear night and the moon's light reflected on the water, making it resemble molten metal and the sand glowed like platinum dust.

'Shall we?' he asked.

They walked onto the sand and removed their shoes, then wandered down to the sea. When it touched her toes, she inhaled sharply, but she kept going until the water was up to her ankles. The chill wrapped around her, making her feel alive and awake, and perfectly present in the moment.

'Rosa,' Henry said, turning her in his arms. 'I'm sure you realise this by now, but I have feelings for you. I care about you and I … I think more. My feelings for you are growing, and I'm wondering if you feel the same.'

His eyes scanned her face, and she sucked in a shaky breath.

'I have feelings for you too,' she said. 'But it's complicated.'

'Because of your childhood?'

'Yes, and because of my life before I came here. I know that you're a kind man and I know you care for me, but I'm still so scared.'

'Let me show you that you can trust me. We can learn together how to put faith in each other and in us. If you want that?' His face was open and earnest and her heart fluttered with emotion, because the last thing she would ever want would be for him to get hurt.

'I want that too.' She reached up and caressed his cheek.

He lowered his head and kissed her and she sighed into him, breathed in his scent of cinnamon and ginger, of caramel and tequila, of mint and geranium. She wanted to hold his scent in her nose and to taste him over and over again. He was delicious, and she longed to give herself to him completely. An ache filled her, to memorise every inch of him with her lips, her fingers, her whole being. It wasn't just desire; it was a longing to surrender, to give herself to him fully—not just physically, but with everything she was.

When she opened her eyes, she knew she owed it to him and to herself to try.

'Life used to feel so full of possibilities,' she said. 'And then it didn't.'

He waited. Didn't push her to say more.

The sea whispered against the shore, its movement as slow and steady as a beating heart. The moonlight shimmered on the water, the sand, and their skin. She had the sense that something was unfolding here, and it was always meant to be this way.

'I ... I was married.' She held her breath, but he nodded, nothing but compassion in his gaze. 'He ... he hurt me a lot. Betrayed me. It ... it makes it so difficult to trust again. I gave him everything, and he took me for a fool.'

'I'm sorry. He was wrong to hurt you and betray you. I am so sorry for what you went through.' Henry stroked her cheeks, her lips, her collar bones then kissed her where his fingers had touched her skin.

'You're not him. You're very different.'

'I love you, Rosa,' he said, his pupils dilating so his eyes seemed black. 'There. I've said it.'

'You do?' she asked. 'Are you sure?'

'I am sure. More certain of it than I've ever been about anything. Although I'm flawed in many ways, my desire is to make you happy. I want to give you everything you want and to fill your life with love. I want to marry you and have a family with you...'

He kissed her again, and she tried to relax into the kiss, but something he'd said nagged at her like a burn. Henry wanted to marry her and to have a family with her. Such easy words to say and yet they were charged with meaning beyond what some people understood. She'd heard the words before and believed in them, trusted in them, and then she had been left broken.

She pulled away from his kiss and placed a hand on his chest. It felt like the air had thickened, refusing to fill her lungs. Panic clawed at her throat.

'What is it?' he asked, his eyes filled with concern. 'Did I say the wrong thing?'

'No. Yes. Oh … I don't know.' She shook her head. She needed to get away from him.

To think. To breathe. To listen to what her mind was telling her about the situation because when she was near him it was hard to think clearly.

She waded out of the water, grabbed her shoes then marched in the direction of the village.

'Rosa?'

She turned. He was still standing in the water. The moon-light limned his body and he looked like he'd just come from the sea — ethereal, otherworldly, too good to be real.

'I'll call you. Please … don't follow me. I need … some space.'

She turned away and hurried up the sand and when she reached the pavement, she slid her feet into her shoes and jogged home. The sand grated against her skin but she didn't care. The discomfort was nothing compared to the pain in her chest. She felt she may even deserve it because she had let things come this far with Henry when she knew, deep down, that she didn't have the right to lead him on.

Rosa's heart was too damaged to love. It was shut down to possibility. Shut down to risk.

She simply couldn't take a chance on Henry because if she did, and he hurt her, she would never recover. Resilience could only carry her so far.

When she reached the bookshop, she let herself inside, then locked the door and sank to the floor. As the tears flowed, she hugged her knees to her chest and surrendered to the pain.

If only Henry Clay had come into her life with his kindness, handsome face, and ability to make her smile before she was broken. If only she hadn't met him now, after she'd already decided she couldn't let anyone in. If only she could move on from the pain and learn to love again.

If only...

25

HENRY

*H*enry trudged through the village. It had been a week since he'd attended the Halloween party with Rosa, and he couldn't believe he hadn't seen her since then. Well, not seen her up close, that was, because they lived in a small village. He'd seen her in the shop, at the café and on the beach, but he'd done his best to stay out of her way. The last thing he wanted was to make her feel there was any pressure from him. He knew what that was like, had been on the receiving end of pressure, and it wasn't what he wanted for himself or for Rosa. She had asked him to give her space, and that was what he would do.

And this even though he was desperate to speak to her, to ask her what had changed when they'd been down at the beach. To find out if he had said or done something to make her have such a dramatic change of heart. Things had been going so well. They'd had a lovely evening, and he'd felt like things between them were progressing. But then he'd said or done something and it was like a switch had flipped inside her and she'd shut down and left him. As she'd walked away, he'd longed to cry out to her, to beg her to stay, but he'd known that would be wrong. Rosa had needed to stretch her wings and fly away, and she had every right to do so.

Henry had gone to work, had got through the days, had done his best to put his sadness from his mind. It was difficult, though, when he had felt so connected to Rosa. They also had Christopher to think about, and Henry had tried to visit him when Rosa wasn't there, when he knew she'd be at work. Christopher had asked if everything was OK, had patted Henry's hand and told him that everything would be all right. Henry didn't know if Rosa had said anything to Christopher about her feelings, but he knew Christopher wouldn't break her confidence if she had.

He wiped a hand over his brow now. Despite the chilly November morning, he felt very warm after his morning run. He was trying to keep in his routine, to stay above the sense of loss for something that had barely just begun, but it wasn't easy. He was off work today since it was Saturday, so he couldn't distract himself with school, but he could visit Christopher and bring him breakfast. Perhaps he'd see if the elderly man wanted to go to the café to eat. It could be nice for him to have a change of scenery.

He'd pop home and shower, then go to Christopher's and see what he wanted to do. Staying busy was the only way he was going to get through this strange time. He hoped Rosa would soon want to speak to him, but until she did, he needed to sit tight. She had to make the next move, so he'd wait to hear from her.

26

ROSA

*I*t was a bright but cold November morning and Rosa was in the shop. She'd opened up an hour ago but felt restless, so when Vinnie arrived, she asked him to watch things. She felt the need to see Christopher and check on him.

'I'll be back in an hour,' she said to Vinnie.

'No problem.' Vinnie nodded as she left the bookshop and walked out into the cold.

Wrapping her scarf around her neck, she strode along the pavement. The sky was navy blue and clouds were being whipped along like trails of smoke by the brisk breeze. She knew the gunmetal grey sea would be freezing cold today and imagined wading into it and plunging beneath the waves to try to get rid of the ache in her heart. The thought sent a shiver running down her spine, and she tucked her hands into her pockets.

Since Halloween, she hadn't spoken to Henry, and she felt sick every time she thought about it. She had behaved badly in running away and not giving him an explanation, but the shame of what had happened to her in her marriage was dreadful. How could she share the truth and see Henry's eyes cloud over? See him realise that if her husband, the man who had sworn to love and protect her for the rest of their lives in their wedding vows, had hurt her so badly, then she surely wasn't worthy of love. Because that was how she'd felt after it had happened and she'd found out what had been going on. She'd put her trust in her ex and he had betrayed her in the worst ways possible. He had acted as though her hopes and dreams, her feelings, were of no consequence to him and, like she was worthless. And that was how she had felt — utterly worthless, and it had taken a long time to try to convince herself otherwise. Surely, if she told Henry about what her husband had done, it would change how he looked at her. He would deny it, but it would plant a seed of doubt and he would wonder why her husband hadn't thought she was worthy of honesty and fidelity. It was better to leave things the way she had than to try to convince herself that Henry could really love her and want a future with her. What if she believed him, believed in them, and then he changed his mind? What if he hurt and deceived her, leaving her with nothing again? It would be more than she could bear and so it was better to face the pain now rather than later. At least now she hadn't been taken for a fool.

Fool me once and all that...

When she got to Christopher's, she knocked on the door then used the key he had given her to let herself in. He'd said he wanted her to have a key just in case there was an emergency and that she was to use it when she came to see him. He'd told her he'd given Henry a key too and she'd nodded but stayed quiet. It made sense for them both to have keys, but she tried to avoid being there when she thought Henry could be visiting.

She called out as she entered his home and waited. A bark echoed from inside the house, but Christopher remained silent, prompting her second call.

Bobby shot through the hallway from the direction of the kitchen and pawed at her leg, so she crouched down and stroked him.

'What is it, boy?'

He barked again, then ran towards the kitchen.

Unease filled Rosa, and she hurried after the small dog, hoping everything was OK.

When she entered the kitchen, she looked around and spotted him.

The world seemed to stop turning, and she froze as she looked at his inert form on the floor next to the Aga. He was wearing his brown cardigan and beige trousers, his checked shirt, and the battered old corduroy slippers that he refused to replace because Dolly had bought them for him.

'Christopher?' she breathed. 'It's me. Rosa.'

Bobby was sitting next to Christopher, pawing at his chest.

'It's OK, Bobby,' she said, even though she didn't think it was OK at all.

She pulled her phone from her pocket and crossed the kitchen, then knelt next to her friend. Placing a hand on his chest, she waited.

A sob caught in her throat, and she typed in 999 on her phone, then waited for the call to connect.

2 7

HENRY

'Hello?' Henry called as he opened the front door and let himself inside. 'It's me, Henry. I've come to see if you fancy going—'

His words trailed away as he looked at the scene in the kitchen.

'Rosa?'

She looked up from Christopher and his heart sank at her red eyes, her blotchy cheeks and at Christopher lying on the floor. Bobby was curled up next to his master. He looked up at Henry but didn't move apart from a small wag of his tail.

'Henry! Please help. The ambulance is on the way.'

He dashed to her side and knelt next to her, touched a hand to Christopher's neck.

'He's alive,' he said, relief rushing through him. 'But he's cold. I'll get blankets.'

Henry ran through to the hallway and unlocked the door for when the paramedics arrived, then went to the lounge and grabbed the crocheted blankets off the back of the sofa. In the kitchen, he wrapped them carefully around Christopher then stroked his forehead.

'Come on, Christopher. You'll be OK. We're here with you and Bobby.' Christopher's eyelids flickered and a ray of hope stirred in Henry. 'That's it, Christopher. Stay with us.'

Rosa covered her mouth with a hand, and he heard her gulp. He wrapped an arm around her shoulders and hugged her to him.

'It will be OK,' he said, and she peered up at him through tear-filled eyes. She looked terrified, and he wished he could take away her fears. But right now, all they could do was wait.

A voice came from Rosa's phone and she replied to it. The call handler was still on the line and was letting her know the ambulance was seconds away.

Soon, there was a knock at the door, and the emergency team entered the kitchen. Henry helped Rosa to stand, and he picked Bobby up, then they moved out of the way while the paramedics performed their assessment. Rosa and Henry answered their questions, and then Rosa asked if she could go in the ambulance with Christopher.

It felt like years were passing while it happened, but it was only minutes, and soon, Christopher was strapped to the stretcher and covered with a blanket. Rosa climbed into the ambulance, and they drove away. Henry locked up the house, then took Bobby to the bookshop. He would ask Vinnie to watch the small dog while he went to join Rosa.

He went into automatic pilot while he drove, unable to let the fear that Christopher would pass away consume him or he would fall apart, and right now, Rosa and Christopher needed him. There would be time enough to let his sorrow consume him later. For now, he had to be strong for the people he loved.

ROSA

*P*acing the waiting room, Rosa hugged herself. Despite her thick jumper and coat she was chilled to the bone. Finding Christopher on the floor had been a shock, and she'd been terrified that he was gone. He was in the best place right now and she tried to reassure herself of that fact, but she also knew that he was frail and elderly and that there was something very wrong. He had collapsed and right now the medical staff were performing tests to find out why.

When the door opened, she turned, expecting to see the doctor, but it was Henry. She sagged as he walked towards her and when he opened his arms; she fell into them.

She cried against his chest, felt him holding her up, and she was more grateful than she could have imagined that he was there with her.

'Any news?' he asked.

'Not yet. They're … still performing tests. Oh Henry, if anything happens to him…'

'I know,' he said. He didn't convince them that Christopher would be fine. He let her know he understood, and that he felt the same. Christopher was their friend, and they cared about him. They wanted the best for him and if they could, of course they would will him to live, but they had no control over this now. All they could do was wait and see. 'Have you let Vinnie know what's happening?'

She nodded. 'I messaged him ten minutes ago.'

'I left Bobby with him. The poor boy was scared, so I couldn't leave him home alone at Christopher's, and I couldn't bring him here.'

'He'll be OK with Vinnie.'

She pulled a tissue from her pocket and dried her eyes and cheeks. Since she'd found Christopher, she'd been going through a cycle of crying, drying her eyes and then crying some more. She'd tried to stop the tears, but it seemed pointless because her pain needed to come out. But now, thankfully, she wasn't alone because Henry was here.

They sat on the blue plastic chairs and Henry took her hand between his and rubbed it to warm it up. She leant against him, let herself rely on him in this moment because she needed his support and friendship. In return, she would offer him hers.

'Are you OK?' she asked.

'Deeply worried for our friend. I just hope they can help him.'

'Henry … I'm so sorry.' She looked up at him, traced the lines of his jaw, his nose, his smooth forehead with her eyes.

'It's not your fault,' he said.

'No … Not about Christopher…' She inhaled deeply as she tried to gather her strength. The room smelt of pine disinfectant and coffee from the machine in the corner. It was stuffy and silent, apart from the humming of a generator somewhere nearby. 'I'm sorry for walking away from you.'

'Hey … Don't do this to yourself. It doesn't matter. Christopher is what matters now.'

She gazed into his blue-green eyes that seemed darker now, more like a pool in a cave than Caribbean waters. Their pain, sadness, and worry pierced her heart like a knife.

'It matters. I need to explain. Is that OK?'

'Of course,' he said. 'I'm listening.'

'I care about you, Henry, more than care about you, but I'm such a mess. I seem like I have my life together, but there are things that happened before I moved to Cornwall, and when they come back to haunt me, I struggle.'

He nodded but didn't speak, and she knew he was giving her space to continue.

'My ex … Zane West… He hurt me badly. I loved him, trusted him and believed in us and he trampled all over that. It made me feel worthless, and I didn't want you to know what he'd done because…' She swallowed against the lump in her throat. 'I … didn't want you to think he was right.'

'Rosa … How could I ever think that anyone who has hurt you is in the right? You are wonderful and the fact that some idiot hurt you makes my blood boil. He clearly didn't deserve you.' Henry shook his head and his eyes shone. He stroked her cheek with his free hand and held her gaze. 'You are the most incredible person I have ever met.'

'I don't know why you think that.' She sucked in a shaky breath. 'I don't understand why you like me so much.'

'There are many reasons…' He smiled then leant closer and kissed her.

When he sat back again, she bit her lip before continuing.

'Our divorce was finalised before I moved here, but I had to pay him off. With some of the money from the sale of my aunt's house. I just wanted him out of my life for good and so I paid him to give me peace.'

'I'm so sorry.'

'Things were OK between us for the first few years we were together. It was fun and easy and he made me laugh a lot. After we got married, we talked about having children. He … he made me believe he loved me and that he wanted to start a family with me. When it didn't happen, I went for tests and so did he. Or he told me he'd been for tests, but he was lying. Mine came back clear, and he said his had too, but it was all part of an elaborate deception. There was no reason for him to lie, but I think he enjoyed it. It was like he couldn't help himself and the lies just rolled off his tongue. See … He'd had a vasectomy. He went away on what he told me was a work trip and during that time he had the vasectomy.' She shook her head as the pain of the memories came back. 'It was like some kind of power play with him because he didn't need to lie, but he did. I know he has issues, and that's the root cause of his behaviour, but even so, it hurt me so much. I thought we were trying for a family, but he took that chance away from me. And with me losing my mum so young and not seeing my dad, I longed for my own family. I wanted to create that unit for myself, to have children and to be a mum and…' A sob choked her and she buried her face in her hands. The fear for Christopher and the sadness from her marriage all washed over her and she couldn't hold it together any longer. She sobbed and sobbed and Henry rubbed her back, held her hands and kissed her hair. When she could breathe again, she continued. 'He was a truck driver, so he was often away and what I didn't know was that he was having affairs. He had women all over the country and they had all fallen for his stories and his charm. I'd never checked up on him, but the last time he was away, a letter came through for him and I opened it by mistake. It was an outstanding bill for the vasectomy and that made me mad. I did some investigating, and that was when I found emails and phone bills for phones I didn't even know he had. He was living several lives and spending money like it was water. He was broke and in debt and that was why, after we divorced, I paid him off to leave me alone. I knew he'd never give me any peace if I didn't.'

'I'm so sorry that happened to you,' Henry said. 'And that I was insensitive mentioning wanting a family with you. After you'd been through that, it was no wonder that it upset you.'

'You weren't insensitive. You were being wonderful. You were offering me everything I ever wanted. I'm so sorry I walked away like that. I should have spoken to you.'

Henry shook his head. 'Sometimes it's hard to form the words we need in order to share the details of our pain. Sometimes, it's not the right time and for you, it wasn't. Now is that time and you have shared your reasons for feeling the way you do.'

'Thank you for understanding.'

'No thanks necessary. And … just so you know… It doesn't make me think less of you. In fact, I think more of you for getting through all that and still being such a sweet and caring person. You are strong and awesome beyond belief. I have nothing but admiration for you. And … other feelings, but I don't want to dump those on you right now.'

'Dump away.' She smiled. 'I adore you, Henry.'

When he kissed her, she melted against him and knew that she had been right to tell him what she was feeling and to share what she had been through. Henry was amazing, and he hadn't judged her, nor had he sided with Zane. He had her back and, it seemed, he wanted to be with her.

'Well…' He smiled at her. 'I stand by what I said to you at the beach. I meant every word. If you want me and a life with me, Rosa, I'm yours.'

She gazed into his eyes, her heart racing, and her love for him filling her up and making her whole again.

But then the door opened, the doctor walked in and she froze as terror reared its ugly head. The doctor closed the door behind her and Rosa thought she would faint with fear, but Henry squeezed her hand then wrapped his big, strong arm around her shoulders.

She knew that whatever happened from here on in, she would be OK as long as this wonderful man was by her side.

EPILOGUE - ROSA

'How's that?' Rosa asked.

'Very comfortable, thank you.' Christopher smiled at her.

'Are you sure you're warm enough?' Henry asked, a small line marring the space between his brows.

'Plenty. Now please, the pair of you, stop fussing.'

'Anyone would think they'd never taken an old man out in a wheelchair before.' Vinnie winked then he knelt down and checked Bobby's winter coat was properly fastened for the tenth time that morning.

A week after being admitted to hospital, Christopher had been allowed to return home. The diagnosis was not good, but they were all coming to terms with it. Tests had found that Christopher had lung cancer, and it seemed he'd had it for some time. He'd attributed his tiredness and occasional breathlessness to his age and not wanted to bother anyone by telling them he had some discomfort when lying down flat.

He had passed out that morning in the kitchen because he was dehydrated, a symptom that the cancer had caused. The medical team listed a range of possible cancer treatments, but Christopher insisted on only palliative treatment, including symptom and pain management, and rejected invasive surgery or gruelling chemotherapy. He said he felt lucky to have reached his nineties and if it was his time, then it was his time.

Henry, Rosa, and Vinnie had spoken at length about the diagnosis, but knew that it was Christopher's choice and that they had no right to dismiss his feelings on the matter. And so they had agreed to support him for as long as they could, and that was what they were doing. Persuading him to use a wheelchair had taken some doing, but he'd been out in it a few times now and he was happy that it would improve his quality of life. He'd admitted to struggling to walk far recently but told them he hadn't wanted to lose his independence and so he had kept it quiet and carried on.

This morning they were heading up to The Garden Café for a little celebration, but they were stopping at the beach first so Bobby could have a run. Rosa and Henry had decided that now Christopher was home, it was time to make the most of every day.

While they walked, Henry pushed the wheelchair, and Rosa walked at his side. Vinnie and Bobby were ahead of them, but Bobby kept stopping to turn and check that Christopher was right behind them. His devotion to Christopher made Rosa's heart ache, and she hoped that the small dog would be OK. She'd promised Christopher that, no matter what, she would love and care for Bobby, and that he would always have a home with her.

Henry glanced at her and smiled, and it warmed her right through. Following a discussion with the doctor at the hospital, they'd been allowed to see Christopher, and they'd sat with him for an hour and held his hands. He'd been so pleased to see them and very grateful that they had found him when they had. His primary concern though, had been for Bobby and how stressful it must have been for the dog when he had passed out.

Rosa, Henry, and Vinnie had agreed that Christopher was not be left alone for long and they'd devised a timetable between them to ensure that one of them was always with him or at least nearby. They were conscious of wanting to be supportive but also to allow Christopher to be independent because he valued that highly, and had been stubborn in his refusal when they'd broached the subject of having carers come in too. He'd said he was well enough to wash and dress himself and would do so for as long as he was able and they'd had to agree that he was.

When they reached the beach, Henry parked the wheelchair next to a bench and put the brake on. Vinnie took Bobby down to the sand and unclipped his lead, then he threw the ball he'd brought for Bobby.

'Ahhh … Look at him go!' Christopher said as he watched Bobby's joy. 'I love watching him play like this.'

'He's adorable.' Rosa nodded.

'Tea?' Henry had got the flask out of his rucksack, and he poured them all a drink, then handed Christopher one.

'This is the life.' Christopher sipped his tea and gazed out at the beach.

Rosa shuffled across the bench so she was sitting right by Henry, and he took her free hand and held it tight. She loved it when he did this, as naturally as if he'd been doing it his whole life. He was such a kind man, and he was, day by day, restoring her faith in love and giving her hope that she could look forward to a future with him.

After half an hour of playing, Bobby, and Vinnie returned to them and they gave Bobby some water, then walked up to the café. The air was fresh but they were all wrapped up in hats, gloves, and warm coats, and Christopher had three blankets around him to ensure that he stayed cosy.

'There you go,' Rosa held open the gate so Henry could push the wheelchair through, then she waited for Vinnie and Bobby to follow before going through herself. They were like a family unit, she often thought, looking out for one another with love and support.

Inside the café, Rosa went to the counter and Pearl greeted her with a smile, then she came around and hugged her.

'Everything ready?' Rosa asked.

'All ready, my dear.' Pearl gave an exaggerated wink, then she went through the door to the kitchen and Rosa joined Henry, Christopher, Vinnie, and Bobby at the table by the green leather sofa.

They removed all their layers and then Rosa handed Christopher a menu. 'See what you fancy,' she said.

When Ellie and Pearl came through the kitchen door, Henry nudged her and she said, 'Oh my goodness! Whatever have you got there?'

They all turned and Pearl said, 'One. Two. Three!'

She walked towards them holding the birthday cake with lit candles and frosted cream icing.

'Happy Birthday to you!' They all sang along as Christopher gaped at them, his mouth open and eyes wide. When he realised what was happening, tears filled his eyes and Rosa got up and hugged him tight.

Pearl set the cake down on the table just as they finished singing.

'How did you … How did you know?' Christopher asked, wiping at his eyes with a tissue Rosa had given him.

'I saw it on the calendar in the kitchen,' Rosa explained. The calendar was from three years ago, but Christopher had kept it because it was from the year he'd lost his wife. Dolly had filled in all their significant dates on it so Rosa had known Christopher's birthday was coming up. 'Happy 93rd Birthday!'

Christopher looked at the candles and said, 'I don't think I have the capacity to blow them all out.'

'I'll help you.'

They blew them out together and then Pearl cut the cake into slices and handed them around on the small plates Ellie had brought from the kitchen.

As they ate the cake and drank tea, Rosa looked at her new family. Her heart brimmed with happiness and love and she knew that from here on, everything would be OK.

She had friends. She had her dream bookshop. She had Henry's love. And she had a new beginning in Cornwall.

She'd been to rock bottom, and now she was on cloud nine.

When you have love, you have everything, she thought, as Henry took her hand and kissed the palm.

And here she was after a wonderful autumn, celebrating with her family at The Cornish Garden Café, and looking forward to extending that family with Henry.

*G*et ready to continue this gorgeously uplifting series with Winter at The Cornish Garden Café

*W*ANT MORE?

Visit my website here - https://rachelgriffith sauthor.com to subscribe to my newsletter, to download free short stories and find out what's next.

Like my Amazon page here https://www.amazon.co.uk/ stores/author/B0716H4KXG to receive alerts about new books and deals.

Take a look at *Also by Rachel Griffiths* for plenty more delightfully uplifting stories!

DEAR READER,

Thank you so much for reading *Autumn at The Cornish Garden Café*. I hope you enjoyed reading the story.
I would be very grateful if you'd leave a rating and a short review sharing your thoughts and feelings about the story.
Stay safe and well!
With love always,
Rachel X

ACKNOWLEDGMENTS

Firstly, thanks to my gorgeous family. I love you so much!

To my friends, for your support, advice and encouragement.

To my AWESOME readers, thank you so much for reading my stories and supporting me with so much love and kindness. XXX

ABOUT THE AUTHOR

Rachel Griffiths is an author, wife, mother, Earl Grey tea drinker, gin enthusiast, dog walker and fan of the afternoon nap. She loves to read, write and spend time with her family.

WANT MORE?

Visit my website here - https://rachelgriffith sauthor.com to subscribe to my newsletter, to download free short stories and find out what's next.
Like my Amazon page here https://www.amazon.co. uk/stores/author/B0716H4KXG to receive alerts about new books and deals.
Take a look at *Also by Rachel Griffiths* for plenty more delightfully uplifting stories!

ALSO BY RACHEL GRIFFITHS…

Cwtch Cove Series
Christmas at Cwtch Cove
Winter Wishes at Cwtch Cove
Mistletoe Kisses at Cwtch Cove
The Cottage at Cwtch Cove
The Café at Cwtch Cove
Cake And Confetti at Cwtch Cove
A New Arrival at Cwtch Cove

A Cwtch Cove Christmas (A collection of books 1-3)

The Cosy Cottage Café Series
Summer at The Cosy Cottage Café
Autumn at The Cosy Cottage Café
Winter at The Cosy Cottage Café
Spring at The Cosy Cottage Café
A Wedding at The Cosy Cottage Café

A Year at The Cosy Cottage Café (The Complete Series)

<u>The Little Cornish Gift Shop Series</u>
Christmas at The Little Cornish Gift Shop
Spring at The Little Cornish Gift Shop
Summer at The Little Cornish Gift Shop

The Little Cornish Gift Shop (The Complete Series)

<u>Sunflower Street Series</u>
Spring Shoots on Sunflower Street
Summer Days on Sunflower Street
Autumn Spice on Sunflower Street
Christmas Wishes on Sunflower Street
A Wedding on Sunflower Street
A New Baby on Sunflower Street
New Beginnings on Sunflower Street
Snowflakes and Christmas Cakes on Sunflower Street
The Cosy Cottage on Sunflower Street
Snowed in on Sunflower Street
Springtime Surprises on Sunflower Street
Autumn Dreams on Sunflower Street
A Christmas to Remember on Sunflower Street
Secret Santa on Sunflower Street
Starting Over on Sunflower Street
The Dog Sitter on Sunflower Street
Autumn Skies Over Sunflower Street
Christmas Magic on Sunflower Street

A Year on Sunflower Street (Sunflower Street Books 1-4)

<u>Standalone Stories</u>
Christmas at The Little Cottage by The Sea
The Wedding

<u>The Cornish Garden Café Series</u>

Spring at the Cornish Garden Café
Summer at the Cornish Garden Café
Autumn at the Cornish Garden Café
Winter at the Cornish Garden Café
A Wedding at The Cornish Garden Café

AUTUMN AT THE CORNISH GARDEN CAFÉ

THE CORNISH GARDEN CAFÉ
BOOK THREE

RACHEL GRIFFITHS

COSY COTTAGE BOOKS

To my found family, I love you all!

CONTENTS

Printed in Dunstable, United Kingdom